"Don't apologize!"
Linc snapped

"Don't bother with excuses, either," he advised in a milder tone. "As you pointed out before, you can't help it."

"I'm not making excuses! The gauge was broken," Allie declared hotly.

He smiled down at her, gently but with a flavor of mockery. "Look, don't let it bother you. There's not much anyone can do but accept the limitations they were both born with. At least you're beautiful enough not to need too many brain cells to get by on."

Allie stared at him as the full import of his words sank in. He really thought she was stupid! Perhaps she ought to explain to this fellow just exactly who she was. Then she realized what else he'd said.

He'd called her beautiful!

Sandra K. Rhoades began reading romance novels for relaxation when she was studying for her engineering degree and became completely hooked. She was amazed at how much fun the books are, and before long her sights were set on a career in romance writing. Colorado-born, she now lives in British Columbia with her husband and their two children. There she raises livestock, and every summer keeps a large garden.

Books by Sandra K. Rhoades

HARLEQUIN PRESENTS

Foolish Deceiver

Sandra K. Rhoades

Harlequin Books

TORONTO • NEW YORK • LONDON
AMSTERDAM • PARIS • SYDNEY • HAMBURG
STOCKHOLM • ATHENS • TOKYO • MILAN

Original hardcover edition published in 1989
by Mills & Boon Limited

ISBN 0-373-03030-4

Harlequin Romance first edition January 1990

To Susan Bates,
with many thanks
for all her help
and advice.

CHAPTER ONE

LOST in thought, Allie Smith didn't notice the slowing of the car until it had nearly come to a halt.

Consequently, it was too late for her to steer it to the side of the road and it stalled in the traffic lane. Fortunately there were few cars travelling along this winding back road on Vancouver Island.

A quick survey of the dials before her revealed nothing amiss. She occasionally forgot about stopping for petrol, but she could see she still had a quarter of a tank. Dismissing that possibility as the reason for her unexpected halt, Allie left the car to inspect the engine.

It started to rain.

Swearing softly to herself, she braced herself against the door while she studied the boxes and suitcases jammed into the back seat and tried to remember which one held her raincoat. She finally recalled that it was in her overnight case in the trunk. Slamming the car door with some violence—rain was starting to trickle down her neck—she walked two paces towards the back of the car, then stopped. Her keys were still in the ignition. She turned back and pulled the handle on the driver's side door. Nothing happened, and she saw that the knob for the door-lock was depressed. She must have pushed it down without noticing when she clambered from the car.

The other door was locked as well.

Pursing her lips in frustration, she treated the

vehicle to a dirty look, then went to look at the engine before working out how she was going to get back into the car. It didn't matter whether she wore a slicker now, anyway. She was already soaked.

With the bonnet raised, Allie stared down at the conglomeration of metal that made up the motor of the car. Internal combustion engines were not difficult to understand, and she knew that automobiles operated on a simple four-stroke cycle. However, the schematic drawings she was familiar with didn't seem to have much in common with all the hoses, belts and lumps of steel that confronted her.

Allie almost didn't hear the sound of the approaching vehicle over the sound of the rain battering on the metal bonnet of the car. When she did hear it, she straightened and saw a dark Ford sedan rounding the curve. Lifting her arm to wave, Allie moved around the car to stand by the driver's side door. There was a squeal of tyres on wet tarmac as the approaching driver slammed on the brakes.

The black Ford Granada skidded to a halt a hair's breadth from the rear of her Pontiac 6000. Before Allie could react, its door was thrust open and a big, dark-haired man emerged.

He stalked up to her. 'You picked a hell of a place to park, lady! You're damn lucky I didn't plough into the back end of you!'

Allie blinked up at him through the rain. His face had a curious grey cast to it, though as she met the murderous glare of his dark eyes it was being washed away by his flush of anger.

She moistened her lips. 'There was room to go around my car,' she offered in defence.

'Sure,' he retorted sarcastically, 'with you standing

in the middle of the road ready to dash out in front of me!'

Although she'd been standing on the traffic side of her parked car, it had hardly been the middle of the road! She was tempted to argue, then decided against it on taking further note of his expression. To put it mildly, he didn't seem to be in a very good mood.

'My car stalled,' she said, bringing the conversation around to the problem at hand.

He didn't reply, although he glanced at the stationary grey coupé. He then looked pointedly to the side of the road, before turning back to her. There was a wide grassy shoulder along this section of road, wide enough to park two cars abreast and still be off the road.

Allie opened her mouth to offer an explanation, then closed it again without speaking. Until quite recently, she'd been barely aware of her habit of letting her mind wander along more interesting paths while mechanically performing routine tasks. She was aware that it was an inconvenience, of course. Her meals were frequently overcooked, her clothes didn't always match, she missed appointments. However, she wasn't your common-or-garden variety daydreamer. Given the calibre of her thoughts, the ideas she had developed when ostensibly involved in something else, a few annoyances had seemed a small price to pay.

Although, in this instance, she *had* been merely wool-gathering, she realised. Her thoughts had been of Kevin, of that last meeting with him . . .

An impatient movement from the man before her recalled Allie to her present predicament. 'I don't know what's wrong with it,' she told him, gesturing to the stationary Pontiac.

'Have you got fuel?' He didn't have to be so sarcastic! she thought, finally goaded into temper. However, it had been quite some time since her car had stopped, and his had been the only vehicle to come along. It probably wouldn't be too wise to send him off with a flea in his ear when he might be able to help her.

She nodded curtly. 'I checked that. I was just having a look under the bonnet when . . .'

'I'll have a look,' he interrupted her abruptly, and she caught her breath on an angry invective. He wasn't just sarcastic, he was downright boorish! 'We'd better get these vehicles off the road first. I'll pull mine off, then we'll push yours over to the side.'

Without waiting for her response, he strode back to his car and got in. Allie drew a deep breath, dampening her irritation. He was going to assist her, so she guessed she shouldn't complain. It would have been nice, though, if her knight in shining armour hadn't turned out to be about as personable as a constipated wolverine.

She watched him deftly reverse his Granada, then wheel it on to the road shoulder to park well away from the edge of the road. When he climbed out and paused for a moment to push a sodden lock of hair back off his forehead, Allie felt a stab of compunction. He had a right to be annoyed at being forced to stop and help her. He was dressed in a well-tailored business suit, its light grey gabardine turning black across his wide shoulders as the rain soaked it. Allie winced as he skidded slightly in the mud along the side of the road and dark goo curled up the sides of his expensive-looking leather dress-shoes. And he'd promised to look at her greasy engine!

She offered him an apologetic smile as he joined

her, but he ignored it. 'You get in and steer while I push your car,' he ordered, moving to the rear bumper and bracing himself against it in the position to push. When he saw that Allie hadn't moved, he straightened. 'Surely you can manage that much? I can't do both.'

Allie swallowed, aware that embarrassed crimson was starting to creep up her face. As he continued to regard her with undisguised impatience, she knew she might as well come out with it. 'I . . . er . . . accidentally locked the keys in. I can't open the door.'

For a long minute, he simply stared at her in amazement. Allie bravely met his gaze, although she longed for the earth to open and swallow her. His eyes weren't the dark brown she had first thought, but a deep navy blue, and she realised that he was a very good-looking man. His features were deeply etched into the bronze of his face, giving him a slightly forbidding countenance that was none the less compelling. Her heart began to beat faster with an odd excitement, and she found herself smiling tentatively at him.

'You can't have been that stupid,' he said at last, squashing her smile. He leaned over to look through the car window, his eyes skipping over the chaos in the back seat to come to rest on the keys dangling from the ignition. Finally, he looked to Allie again. 'You can't have been that stupid,' he reiterated.

'Well, I'm sorry, but I was,' Allie retorted, her hard tones masking the hurt she was feeling. Nature had endowed her with a brain that could grasp the most complex and abstract thoughts conceived by man; however, when it came to the trivialities of everyday life . . . 'I couldn't help it.'

The stranger gave her a look of impatience, then

swung away from her and started walking back to his car, shaking his head slightly as he went.

Panic swept through her. He couldn't just leave her here! She charged after him, slipping and sliding in the mud as she went. She had nearly caught up with him when her feet shot out from under her and she sprawled face-down into the mud.

He heard her cry out and turned back. 'Good lord, what are you up to now?' he exclaimed, coming back to help her up. 'Why didn't you stay over on the road by the car?' Grasping her forearm, he hauled her to her feet.

'I thought you were going to leave me here,' Allie admitted, brushing gingerly at the mud clinging to the front of her dress. Her palms stung from the harsh contact with the rocky soil, and one knee was starting to throb.

'I wasn't leaving. I was just going to see if I could find a length of wire I could use to open your car door.'

'Oh,' Allie mumbled, feeling foolish for having panicked. His anger seemed to have fled, though, even if he still wasn't exactly friendly. He had retained his hold on her arm, and suddenly she was acutely aware of his touch. She edged slightly away from him and his hand fell away. For some reason, the loss of that warm contact made her conscious of how cold and wet she was. She shivered.

She heard him mutter something under his breath, then he was shrugging off his suit-jacket and holding it out to her. 'Here, put this on before you freeze to death.'

'Oh, I couldn't. I'm all dirty and you . . .'

'Just put it on and don't stand here arguing in the rain,' he grated, thrusting it at her. Allie glanced up and, seeing his expression, clamped her lower lip between her teeth. Meekly accepting the jacket, she shrugged into it as he moved on to the rear of his car and started rummaging in its trunk.

About fifteen minutes later, Allie was seated behind the wheel of her car, steering it to the side of the road while her rescuer pushed it. She had offered to help when he was manoeuvring the wire along the edge of the window to catch the knob on the door-lock, but he'd told her not to bother. Since he seemed in a slightly better mood, she hadn't argued, although she suspected she could have accomplished the feat with less effort—and less swearing. After all, she'd had practice. This wasn't the first time she'd locked herself out of her car.

While the stranger tinkered with the engine, Allie remained behind the wheel, ready to try the ignition whenever he called out to her. As the minutes ticked by, Allie grew restless. The man didn't seem to be making much progress getting the car running, and every once in a while she could hear him muttering to himself.

If only something simple had been wrong with it, she thought restively, she could have been on her way by now. Glancing over the dials in front of her again, she sought a clue to the car's misbehaviour. The gauge still read a quarter of a tank of petrol. She tapped the glass front of the dial thoughtfully. The needle quivered, then to her amazement fell over to below the 'E'.

She stared at it for a moment, then looked up to see the man coming towards her. He was wiping his soiled hands on a rag as he came. His white shirt was soaked, plastering his well-muscled torso in a semi-transparent film. A dark smear of grease decorated one sleeve. Guiltily, Allie laced her fingers together in her lap.

He leaned over to speak to her through the open window. 'We'll have to have it towed to a garage. I can't figure out what the trouble is, and if we keep on trying to start it we'll just end up draining the battery.'

'Well . . . actually, I've just found out it was the fuel all along . . . er—there isn't any.' She could see his features hardening and rushed on, 'The gauge must have been stuck. I tapped it and the needle went to empty. See?' She pointed to the gauge.

When she looked back to him, there was a flush along the top of his cheekbones. His hands were clenched around the rag he'd been using, twisting it together. She had the distinct impression he was wishing it was her neck.

'I'm really sorry about this. I . . .'

'Don't apologise!' he snapped, and she jumped slightly. He gazed down into her wide grey eyes, which were shadowed with guilt, and took a deep, calming breath. A moment passed before it had any effect, then his hands slowly eased their stranglehold on the rag. His expression of anger softened to one of mere exasperation. 'Don't bother with excuses, either,' he advised in a milder tone that was oddly bitter. 'As you pointed out before, you can't help it.'

Allie felt some of the tension easing out of her. 'Well, no, I didn't think to check the gauge . . .'

'No, I'd guessed that blonde hair was natural,' he interposed drily.

She gave him a puzzled glance. She had meant to say she hadn't thought to check to see if the gauge was working properly. His comment didn't seem apropos to that, though. It was almost as if—the light dawned.

'I'm not making excuses! The gauge *was* broken. When I looked at it earlier, it showed a quarter of a tank!' Allie declared hotly.

He smiled down at her, gently but with a flavour of mockery. 'Look, don't let it bother you. There's not much anyone can do but accept the limitations they were born with. At least you're beautiful enough not to need too many brain cells to get by on. Stop apologising.'

Allie stared at him as the full import of his words sank in, her lips parting as her jaw dropped. He really thought she was stupid—a dumb blonde! Ignoring her flabbergasted expression, he continued, 'I've got a hose in the trunk of my car. I'll see if it will work to syphon some fuel from my tank for you—enough to get you to a petrol station, anyway.'

Allie stared at his back as he walked away, dumbfounded by his conclusions about her. Although she was absent-minded about day-to-day affairs, she had never been expected to pay much attention to the mundane details of life. She had been five years old when testing had discovered she possessed an IQ of a hundred and ninety-four. Since that time, her entire life had been geared towards exploiting the potential of that incredible brainpower. She'd received her doctorate at the age of seventeen, the youngest Ph.D. in her university's history. Now, at twenty-four, she was one of the world's most respected experts in the field of computer mathematics.

Only Kevin had ever tackled her about her eccentricities, and then only obliquely. He'd called her a clinging vine because she relied on others to keep her life running on smoothly oiled wheels—and he didn't want the job. However, he hadn't accused her of lacking in intelligence because of her lapses.

She reached for the door-handle to let herself out of the car. Perhaps she ought to explain to this fellow just exactly who she was. However, her hand froze on the handle as she recalled what else he'd said.

He'd called her *beautiful*!

For a moment, Allie sat, stunned, then unconsciously released her grip on the door-handle. She shifted in her seat so that she could see herself in the rear-view mirror. A heart-shaped face; large grey eyes fringed by dark lashes; a small nose that turned up slightly at the end; a wide, full-lipped mouth—she supposed the inventory didn't add up to too bad a picture, but people just didn't tell Dr Allison Jennings Smith she was beautiful! They told her she'd made some very salient points in that last article she'd published, or asked her opinion on the latest theory on whatever—but no one ever told her she was beautiful!

'There's fuel in your tank now—enough to get you to the petrol station that's three or four miles further along this road. Don't push your luck, though. Stop and fill up there.' The man had returned to her side without her being aware of him, and Allie was startled away from the contemplation of her reflection. Swinging her eyes to him, she gave him a wondering look. He'd actually told her she was beautiful, recognised her as a woman—maybe a stupid one, but a woman none the less. That seldom happened in her life. She was a highly developed brain, a super-computer that interfaced with the lesser models she worked on.

'You shouldn't have any trouble finding the service station,' he supplied when Allie remained staring at him in silence. He was frowning impatiently as he gestured to the road in front of them. 'You just stay right on this road and you can't miss it. I'd follow you to make sure you get there all right, but frankly I'd like to be on my way.'

'Oh, yes, of course,' Allie said quickly. 'It was good of you to stop and help me in the first place. I'm sorry for any inconvenience I've caused you. I . . .'

'If I could just have my jacket back?' he asked, damming the flow of her gratitude.

She'd completely forgotten she was still wearing it. Flustered, she fumbled with the door-handle, then thrust the car door open and scrambled out. As she clumsily shrugged out of the jacket to hand it over, she could feel the heat burning in her face, acutely aware that he was waiting impatiently for the return of his property.

However, when she'd handed it over, he didn't move away immediately. She dared an upward glance into his face, her own burning even hotter when she read his look. The jacket had moulded the damp bodice of her dress to her full breasts, and she could feel her nipples hardening in the sudden chill of air. The man's deep navy eyes rested on them, admiring and speculative.

'Well, sorry to have delayed you,' Allie stammered, swinging about and diving back into her car. The ignition fired at a twist of the key, and she slipped the Pontiac into gear. Her rescuer was forced to jump hastily out of her path as she put her foot down on the accelerator.

'I really appreciate your letting me invite myself for a visit,' Allie said. In her dressing-gown, she was curled up on the bed in Clare Evans's guest-room, sipping a mug of steaming hot chocolate as she talked with her hostess. A hot bath had washed away the mud and

rain-chill left over from her adventures earlier in the
day, and she felt warmer and more relaxed than she
had in weeks.

'Don't say another word about it,' Clare
admonished. 'I've been asking you to come see us for
years, but you've always been too involved in this
project or that to get away. Greg and I are delighted
that you were finally able to take us up on our
invitation.'

'Well, I didn't have anything to stop me this time,'
she replied, unable to keep bitterness from colouring
her tones. Clare gave her a considering look and Allie
quickly turned her head to look out of the window.
The rain had stopped, and a watery sun was starting
to emerge from behind the clouds. The front of the
Evanses' house overlooked the Strait of Georgia and
afforded a sweeping view of the seascape. The guest-
room, however, overlooked the back garden, and
beyond it the rain forest. Majestic Douglas fir trees
with rainwashed foliage, tipped with the bright green
of new growth, towered over cedars, their great
looping boughs festooned with honeysuckle. Bright
patches of palest green announced dogwood in bloom,
and the cloying perfume of Saskatoon bushes
permeated the air.

The forest floor was a jungle of vegetation, ferns
and shrubs competing with bushes and young trees. It
would be easy to get lost in there, Allie thought,
wondering if maybe that wasn't what she wanted from
life right now—to lose herself for a while.

'So why aren't you involved in a project right now?'
the older woman asked. Allie turned back to her and
gave her a faint smile, not resenting the probing
question. She'd known Clare since their college days,
and the woman was one of the few friends she'd made

during that period of her life. She'd been so very much younger than everyone else then that it hadn't been easy to make friends. The professors had treated her as something of a freak, and the other students either resented her superior intelligence or dismissed her as a pesky kid.

Clare hadn't reacted in either of those ways. Popular and extrovert, she had been a mediocre student who'd come to university mainly for the social rather than the intellectual opportunities. Five years older than Allie, the fun-loving brunette and the sober, introverted teenager had made an odd pair. However, from their first meeting, Clare had taken the gangling adolescent who'd come to tutor her in first-year mathematics under her wing. She'd been one of the few people to see that, despite her high IQ, Allie had none the less been a lonely child struggling to survive in an adult world.

'I've been making a fool of myself over a man,' Allie blurted out, her mouth twisting in self-disgust.

Although it wasn't funny, Clare smiled faintly, as Allie's expression was so strongly reminiscent of the young girl she had befriended years earlier. Aside from her outstanding brainpower, Allie had always been remarkably conscientious. During college she'd always felt incredibly guilty whenever Clare had coaxed her away from her books in pursuit of something less uplifting—the complete opposite of Clare's own attitude towards studying!

'Well, you're not the first woman to do that!' she assured her, controlling her amusement.

'No, I suppose not,' Allie admitted. She gestured helplessly with her hands, then linked them in her lap and stared down at them.

'So, you got hurt,' Clare murmured sympathetically

Allie sat motionless for several moments before meeting Clare's gaze. 'The pathetic thing is that I don't know if I did or not. I'm angry and my ego's bruised, but, more than anything, I think I'm disgusted with myself for being such a fool!'

'Why don't you tell me about it?'

Allie pushed her hand through her hair, brushing it away from her forehead, before speaking. 'About eight months ago, I got a new assistant at the Institute. His name was Kevin Alderson. Right from the start, we worked really well together. I've had problems in the past with some of the people who've worked under me. If they don't resent me as their chief because I'm a woman, it's because I'm usually much younger than they are. I didn't have any of those problems with Kevin, though.' She shrugged, momentarily falling silent.

'So go on, what happened? Did he make a pass at you?' Clare prompted.

Allie gave her a wry grimace. 'Nothing so obvious. It all started very casually—we worked late one night and he suggested we have dinner together when we'd finished. It got to be a regular thing after a while, then he started asking me out at other times.'

'So you dated him?'

'I know it doesn't sound like a very big deal, but it was to me. I've never had any real social life until I met Kevin. At college I was just a kid, and when I went to work at the Institute I was too busy to worry about having a love-life. Besides, most of the men working there are married or old enough to be my father. Kevin was different, though. He's in his early thirties, good-looking, single—a really eligible bachelor, and I haven't been around those very often. Anyway, to cut a long story short, I started formulating all these big day-dreams about love and marriage and happy-ever-afters, only that wasn't what he was looking for at all.'

Allie fell silent, turning to gaze out of the window again. She suspected she hadn't really loved Kevin, but had been more in love with the *idea* of loving him and making her life with him. Until he'd come along, she hadn't realised just how much she wanted the things other women had: a husband, a home, a family. They had never seemed attainable until Kevin had shown an interest in her. Since he'd left her, that kind of future had moved right back into the realms of the impossible, and she thought maybe that hurt more than his perfidy.

'There must be more to the story than that,' Clare interrupted her thoughts. 'You may be inexperienced, Allie, but with your intelligence you wouldn't build up that kind of expectation from a few dates. He must have given you some encouragement.'

Reluctantly, Allie dragged her eyes from the scene outside and back to her friend. 'I'm ashamed to tell you all the gory details. I was so stupid!'

'Spill it,' Clare coaxed.

'I slept with him!' She held the other woman's eyes for a moment, then dropped her gaze to the spread covering the bed. Distractedly, she fingered one of the tufts of chenille. 'We went to this conference. The booking was for a two-bedroom suite, but we only used one of the bedrooms . . .' She gestured rather helplessly. 'I wish that I could say I was carried away on a tide of passion or something, but I wasn't. Sharing a room with Kevin just seemed the right thing to do. I mean, here I was, a twenty-four-year-old virgin . . . it seemed about time I climbed out of the Victorian era. Only, mentally, I don't think that I did.

I thought because he made love to me that meant he *loved* me—and because I agreed to it, I must love him. I was being hoplessly naïve.' Allie felt a tight band of pain compressing her chest, stifling further speech.

Clare moved to sit on the bed beside her, covering Allie's restless fingers with her own. 'Hey, come on, you obviously didn't force him to make love to you.'

'He hinted at it later,' Allie muttered bitterly.

'What?'

'He suggested I'd blackmailed him into . . . to—er—sleeping with me.' She took a deep breath, forcing back the threatening tears. 'I mean, I was his boss—how could he turn me down?'

'The louse!' Clare exclaimed vehemently. 'He told you this when you got back to the Institute?'

'Not right away. When we first came back, I was still living in a fool's paradise—all starry-eyed and full of plans. I thought . . . I thought that weekend we'd just sort of anticipated marriage . . . I hadn't realised yet that it was nothing but a one-night stand. Anyway, he didn't make love to me again, but we still went out, he took me places. Then, one day, the bomb fell.' The last word caught on a sob and Clare squeezed her hand in comfort. After a few moments, Allie was able to continue. 'I'd been putting together this proposal . . . working out some ideas for a new computer program to be used in the launch system for communications satellites. Once I got the groundwork completed, the Institute was going to put in a bid to Ottawa to develop it, but at this stage it was all very hush-hush. No one was supposed to know any of the details except myself and my supervisor. Anyway, I was indiscreet, and I discussed what I was working on with Kevin. I had the file on it in the computer, and I even called it up one day when Kevin was with me. I never thought about his seeing the access code.'

'So what happened?'

'I was just about ready to present my proposal when we heard that a private firm had obtained the contract for a similar project using a nearly identical approach. Two days later, Kevin came into my office to resign . . . he'd got a new job with the company that had received the contract. He was going to be heading the project.'

She gave Clare an unhappy look. 'Even then, I didn't twig what had happened. Instead, I tackled him about us . . . about all those silly dreams I'd been formulating. This other company was on the other side of the country . . . I didn't want him to leave. We argued, and finally he put it in the plainest terms possible that the only reason he'd gone out with me, made l-love to me . . .' Allie was forced to pause and take a deep breath, 'was because I was his boss, and he thought I could help his career. He admitted that he'd stolen my work to give to this other company in order to get the job with them.'

Her eyes were wide and anguished when she looked at her friend. 'I accepted his resignation then. A few days later, I wrote out my own.'

'Oh, Allie, what did you do that for?' Clare asked, slipping her arms around her shoulders and hugging her. 'You've worked for the Institute since you left university. You needn't have left. Surely . . .'

'It was the only ethical thing for me to do. Once word got around about Kevin's leaving and going to the other company, the rumours started flying. People knew I had been seeing Kevin socially; they also knew we'd just lost a project to this company. It didn't take them long to start putting two and two together.'

'But that still doesn't mean . . .'

'Yes, it does, Clare,' Allie said firmly. 'The rumours were more or less true. Maybe I didn't intentionally hand that information over to Kevin, but the result was the same. Because of my infatuation with him, I cost us what could have been a lucrative contract. My job with the Institute was an important position, a position of trust . . . I violated that trust.'

'I don't think you should have left,' her friend argued. 'It really wasn't your fault that you were taken in by this Kevin. I'm sure you could have explained.'

Allie shook her head, dismissing Clare's arguments. 'At that point, I didn't really care. I wanted to get away from the Institute anyway, to get away from all the people who knew about me and Kevin . . . to get away from being Allison Jennings Smith, B.Sc., M.Sc., Ph.D.!'

Silence filled the room as Allie sat huddled on the bed, blinking back the tears that insisted on gathering in her eyes. Her friend's arm was firm and warm across her back, lending comfort, and after a few minutes she regained control.

'So what are your plans?' Clare asked, letting her arm fall as she saw that Allie was recovering.

The younger girl shrugged. 'I'm not sure. I'd like to stay here for a few days, if you'll have me.' The sun was streaming in the window and once again Allie's eyes were drawn to the view outside. 'This is beautiful country. If I could find a place to rent around here, I wouldn't mind staying the summer. I don't need to look for another job right away.'

'Why don't you stay here, then?'

Allie sighed. 'It's an idea, but I think I'd like to go somewhere where nobody knows me. Somewhere where I wouldn't be Dr Smith and could live as an ordinary person.' She hesitated, nibbling her lower lip. The Institute was located in a small prairie town, and everyone knew her background. She'd never had a chance to be anything other than Dr Allison Smith, brilliant mathematician. The stranger who had helped her with her car earlier that day came into her mind. He'd been churlish, rude—called her stupid, no less!—but he'd also said she was beautiful. He'd seen her as a woman and not some freak of nature—but then, he hadn't known who she was.

'You can do that here,' Clare's voice intruded into her thoughts. 'Greg and I are the only ones who know you. We don't need to advertise your background. In fact . . .' The brunette eyed her thoughtfully for a moment, a speculative gleam lighting her bright blue eyes. 'I think this thing with Kevin hit you so hard because you just don't know anything about men. What you need is some experience!'

'I've just got some,' Allie reminded her sardonically. 'I don't think I'm that keen on rushing out to get any more just yet.'

'But you must!' the older girl declared. 'It's like falling off a horse—if you don't get back on right away you'll lose your nerve. All men aren't like this Kevin, and you just need to find yourself a better one.'

'Life isn't quite that simple, Clare. For one thing, most men don't want anything to do with a woman who's smarter than they are—their egos can't handle it.'

'Then we won't let them know your IQ!' Clare enthused, undeterred by Allie's statement. Her eyes were glowing with excitement as she shifted on the bed to study the other girl's face and figure. 'You've got a lot of potential—you just haven't exploited it. With a little help from me, you're going to become the sexiest bombshell that's ever hit the men of this island. And when they're all swarming about you, I'm not going to let you scare them off with that computer-like brain of yours. You're going to play dumb!'

Allie gave her friend a doubtful look—Clare always did come up with the wildest schemes. 'How am I supposed to carry that off? I'm no actress. I think it's this idea that's dumb.'

'It'll work great, it'll be fun,' Clare insisted. She reached out and fingered a strand of Allie's hair. 'Aren't we lucky that your hair is already blonde?'

The comment startled Allie, reminding her of her rescuer. Maybe Clare's crazy idea would work. After all, one person in the world already thought she was a 'dumb blonde'!

CHAPTER TWO

'I DON'T know about this,' Allie said doubtfully. 'I feel half-naked.' Her fingers tugged at the elasticised neckline of the blouse she was wearing, then released it. It fell back to the top of her bosom, leaving the shadowed cleft between her breasts partially exposed. The revealing peasant blouse was teamed with a narrow-waisted full skirt in a gay floral pattern. The outfit was a far cry from the conservative clothes she favoured, and Allie eyed it with disapproval. It made her look . . . well, voluptuous!

'It looks great,' Clare assured her. 'That outfit is perfect, so don't even think about wearing something else. It has just the right combination of little-girl innocence and sex-kitten that we want.'

While Allie grimaced—sex-kitten!—Clare tucked her tongue into the corner of her mouth and she eyed Allie's face with an artist's intensity. 'Close your eyes again so I can put on a little more eyeshadow.'

Obediently, Allie did as she was told, wondering what Clare would do if she sneaked off and washed her face before going down to the party—or, better yet, skipped the party altogether. Unfortunately, Allie knew she couldn't do it, no matter how much she dreaded being put on display for Clare's bachelor friends. Clare had gone to a lot of trouble arranging this barbecue for her, not the least being clipping and grooming her person over the past week as though she were a prized poodle being prepared for an important show. A poodle wouldn't have been nearly as embarrassed by all the fuss as Allie was, though.

'You can open your eyes now,' Clare said. 'I'll just dab a bit more powder on your nose, then I'll let you turn around and see the result.'

While Clare wielded the powder-puff, Allie mentally prepared herself to praise her friend's efforts—regardless of how awful she looked. Clare was a sweetie and, even if Allie didn't relish presenting herself to a group of strangers decked out like a 'lady of the evening', she wasn't going to hurt her feelings.

Her smile was ready when the other girl swivelled the chair around so Allie could see herself in the mirror. It never made it. Allie was too busy staring at herself in astonishment. Although she'd been convinced that Clare had plastered half the make-up kit on her face, the result was amazingly natural and attractive. The hint of lilac shadow on her lids turned her ordinary grey eyes to a mysterious smoky violet; the mascara made her lashes appear impossibly thick and long. Subtle peach blusher tinted her cheeks, emphasising the perfect bone-structure, and her mouth glowed, soft and inviting, with the addition of creamy lip-gloss. She'd despaired yesterday when Clare had dragged her to the hairdresser to have her long, straight hair trimmed and shaped into a casual, flyaway style. She thought it had looked a mess afterwards. Today, though, she saw the honey-gold locks with new eyes, and realised the new style made her look young and carefree and—sexy.

'So what do you think?' Clare demanded.

Allie tore her gaze away from the stranger in the mirror and looked up at her friend. 'I don't know what to say. It doesn't even look like me.'

Clare grinned. 'Of course it does—the *new* you.

You're going to knock 'em dead!'

Allie turned back to her reflection, half expecting the image to have altered. She'd been incredibly flattered when that strange man had called her beautiful—although in her heart she hadn't really believed him. Studying her face now, though, she decided that there just might be a grain of truth in what he'd said.

She heard Clare sigh, and glanced up to see the other woman watching her. Her expression was very much the same as Michelangelo's must have been after he'd placed the last brushstroke on the ceiling of the Sistine Chapel. Allie felt her lips twitching with amusement.

'I know just the fellow for you,' Clare mused. 'Linc Summerville moved into the neighbourhood last fall. He's a widower, and every single woman and quite a few of the married ones have been chasing him ever since. When he gets a look at you, I think he might just decide to stop running!'

Allie's amusement was pushed out by a creeping chill—probably originating at her feet! Clare's comment brought to the fore just exactly what this transformation was all in aid of. 'You know, Clare,' she began tentatively, 'you did a super job fixing me up, but even though I look better, I don't think I'm the *femme fatale* type. This Linc what's-his-name and all those other single men you've invited to this party . . .' She shook her head. 'Even if they are attracted by the "new me" . . . what am I supposed to do then? I'm not a flirt. I won't know what to say to them.'

'You'll think of something,' Clare assured her blithely. 'Just don't start talking about computers and those algorithm things you're always going on about.'

'But that's what I'm comfortable talking about,'

Allie argued. She glanced back to her reflection and shook her head. 'I've been doing a lot of thinking this past week . . . OK, I went off the deep end over Kevin and started getting a lot of silly ideas about getting married and all that stuff. I went crazy for a little while, but I'm sane now. I really think I should start looking for another job. Despite everything, the Institute did give me a good reference, and I won't have much trouble finding something else. My career is my future, and I need to concentrate on that. I'm not the marrying kind.'

'Don't be such a coward!' Clare enjoined. 'You said you were going to find a place to rent around here and stay for the summer. Don't chicken out now.'

'Can't you see that all this,' she gestured to her image in the mirror, 'is just a waste of time? Suppose some guy does become attracted to me. I can't play the dumb blonde for the rest of my life! What's going to happen when he finds out I've got an IQ of a hundred and ninety-four? He'll drop me flat, because men just don't want to be around women who are smarter than they are. I know from experience.'

'Would you stop being such a pessimist? If he's in love with you, it won't matter.'

'Love conquers all?' Allie asked cynically; however, on seeing Clare's distressed look, she sighed remorsefully. She supposed it wouldn't hurt anything to play along with her friend for a few weeks. Kevin had taught her a valuable lesson, so she knew better than to take anything that might result from Clare's scheming too seriously.

'OK, Clare,' she said at last, smiling faintly. 'I'll give it a try.'

It was just possible that Clare had invited the Seventh

Fleet to her barbecue, Allie decided, gazing about the steam-filled kitchen in wonder. Certainly, judging from the amount of food her friend was preparing for the event, that would be a logical assumption. And all the pots, pans and assorted paraphernalia didn't even include the enormous salmon that was baking on the grill outside!

'Are you sure I can't help you with any of this?' Allie asked, gesturing somewhat helplessly with her hands. She felt guilty about letting Clare carry the entire burden of preparing the food for the party but her own culinary skills were limited.

'Everything's under control. I just have to wait for stuff to cook.' She brushed her hand across her heat-flushed cheek and grimaced. 'Maybe you could watch things for me while I go and freshen up, though. I'm glad the weather has turned out warm, but this hot kitchen has turned my make-up into a blob of grease.'

'Just tell me what you want doing.'

'Not much of anything. All you have to do is make sure nothing boils over or burns. I'll only be a minute.' When Clare reached the door, she paused and looked back over her shoulder to Allie. 'If Greg comes in from mowing the lawn before I get back, tell him to come and get changed. Knowing him, he'll greet our guests in his ratty old cut-offs if we don't nag him.' She turned to leave, then once again turned back. 'Oh! I forgot the salad dressing. The recipe is on that card by the blender. You can throw it together for me, can't you?'

She was out of the room before Allie could respond. Reluctantly, Allie went over to inspect the recipe card lying on the counter. When she'd offered to help, she'd been thinking along the lines of opening cans or something, maybe peeling some vegetables. She could handle that. Keeping things from burning and actually preparing things requiring a recipe weren't her strong points. As her eyes skimmed the list of ingredients for the dressing, she wished Clare had let McDonald's cater for this affair.

However, once she started measuring and pouring things into the blender, Allie discovered following a recipe wasn't that hard. Cooking was a lot like chemistry—only it was easier to measure things in cups and tablespoons than moles! She was actually enjoying her unfamiliar task when Greg came in, and she blithely sent him off to change, confident she could finish the dressing without any hang-ups.

That was perhaps overly optimistic. Having added a final carefully measured teaspoon of salt to the concoction in the blender, Allie put the lid on and pushed down the button that would turn it on. Nothing happened. She checked to see that the machine was plugged in, then lifted off the lid and peered down in frustration at the undisturbed liquid. Damn, things had been going so well, too.

She suddenly realised that the radio that had been playing softly in the background was now silent. Looking along the appliance-loaded counter-top, she realised that the 'on' lights had gone out on the crock-pot and the automatic coffeemaker.

Well, she might not know much about cooking, but electricity was another matter. Her switching on of the blender must have caused an overload and tripped the fuse. She turned off the crock-pot and coffeemaker, then realised she would have to get Greg or Clare to tell her where the fusebox was located.

At that moment, the front doorbell chimes resounded in the silent kitchen—the first of Clare's guests had arrived. Knowing Clare and Greg were busy, she realised she should go and admit them. However, her troublesome feet were rapidly turning to ice as she was assailed by stage-fright. It was going to be difficult enough meeting all those strangers with Clare beside her to ease the introductions. She simply couldn't meet them alone!

When the doorbell sounded a second time, Allie's eyes roamed around the kitchen somewhat desperately. They came to rest on the door leading to the basement stairs. Electrical panels were usually located in basements! Escape beckoned. Although disgusted by her cowardice, Allie none the less headed for the door and shot down the stairs.

It took her only a few moments to discover the fuse panel located a few feet from the base of the stairs. She spent several minutes inspecting the array of switches, even though the tripped switch was obvious at a glance. It wasn't until she heard muffled voices and footfalls coming from the kitchen overhead though that she forced herself to stop procrastinating. She pulled the offending switch to reset it, slightly startled by the sudden increase in the noise coming from overhead. However, refusing to allow herself to use that as an excuse for continuing to hide in the basement, Allie went back up the stairs.

She found Clare and Greg in the kitchen with another couple and, on first impressions, it seemed that everyone was talking at once. Hesitantly, Allie slipped into the room and made for Clare's side.

She never reached it.

'Allie, there you are!' Clare announced as she spotted her. When everyone turned to look at her, Allie self-consciously came to a halt in the centre of the room.

'I tripped the fuse when I turned on the blender and

was just downstairs resetting——' The sentence came
to an abrupt end as Allie recognised her friend's male
guest. It wasn't difficult. She'd know that scowl
anywhere!

'You!' the erstwhile rescuer thundered. 'I should
have guessed!'

Allie cringed slightly. That angry tone of voice
wasn't exactly unfamiliar, either. Eyeing him warily,
she noticed that he looked sort of odd. He wasn't
dripping rain as he had been the other day, but he
looked kind of . . . speckled. Puzzled, Allie stared at
him more closely. Funny little white gobs of
something were splattered over the front of his dark
brown sports shirt. The same substance decorated his
bronze face and even the front strands of his night-
dark hair.

'I . . . er . . .' Allie stammered in confusion as he
glared at her, rendering her unable to pull her eyes
away from his. It was a relief when Clare handed him
a towel and he used it to wipe his face, momentarily
diverting that furious gaze from her. She seized the
opportunity to switch her attention to Clare. 'What
happened?'

'Don't worry about it,' Clare soothed, dabbing at
the man's shirt-front with a paper towel. 'It wasn't
really your fault. It was an accident.'

'Yes, but what happened?'

Clare's ministrations had turned the little white
blobs on the shirt into unattractive dark circles. 'I
think I've only made things worse,' she commented to
her guest, ignoring Allie's question for the moment.
'Greg will lend you a fresh shirt and I'll put this one
in to soak.'

'Clare, will you please tell me what happened?'
Allie demanded.

Clare disposed of the paper towel, then said, 'It really wasn't your fault.' Allie gave her a frustrated look. If that were true, then why did Clare keep repeating it, and why did that man keep looking at her as though he wanted to strangle her? The other woman continued, 'It's the silliest thing, really. I guess you forgot to switch the blender off before you went down to reset the fuse. The lid wasn't on it, so when the power came on again the dressing . . .' She gestured expressively with her hands. 'Unfortunately, Linc was standing right next to it and got in the way.'

Automatically, Allie's eyes swivelled to look at him. The angry scowl had faded and he now wore a look of resignation. 'As Clare said, it was an accident—not your fault,' he admitted on a sigh.

Allie felt herself shrinking inwardly from his patronising regard. He was accepting that it was an accident, but an accident due to her stupidity. He obviously thought that she didn't have the intelligence that God gave a goose. Since Clare had advised her to adopt the image of the dumb blonde, maybe she should have been gratified, but instead she only felt humiliated.

Without further ado, Greg took the other man off to find him another shirt. Allie felt a great deal more comfortable upon his exit and turned to Clare, apologising, 'I'm really sorry about the mess, Clare. I'll get it cleaned up for you.'

'I can take care of it,' the older woman assured her. 'I've got some things to look after in here anyway. Why don't you take Elaine out on to the patio and get her something to drink?' When Allie smiled hesitantly at the other woman in the room, she exclaimed, 'I guess I forgot about introducing you. Elaine, this is my friend Allie Smith. Allie, this Elaine Colridge.

That was Linc Summerville who was just here.'

Allie remembered her earlier conversation with
Clare, and wondered if this was one of the women
who was 'chasing' Linc Summerville. If she was, Allie
figured she needed her head examined. Personally,
she had decided to run the other way if he ever looked
in her direction—not that that was very likely to
happen.

She was a little surprised by her sudden upsurge of
curiosity on meeting one of his girlfriends, though.
She was further surprised to discover that Elaine
Colridge wasn't at all the type of woman she would
have expected him to pick as a lover. When—and
why—had she started speculating on his taste in
women?

Regardless of that, Elaine still wasn't what she was
expecting. Allie's mental image had been of a cool
model type, dripping sophistication and chic. Elaine
Colridge was remarkably ordinary. Her mousy brown
hair, cut in a nondescript style, framed her pale, plain
face. What should have been her best feature—large,
luminous brown eyes—somehow seemed to dwarf the
rest of her features and made her look a little like a
cocker spaniel.

Physically, Elaine was very slender, with a boyish
figure clad in a dark navy trouser-suit which managed
to look staid despite its casualness. In comparison,
Allie felt like an overblown rose in her gay peasant
outfit with her carefully made-up face and 'sex-kitten'
hairdo. As Elaine half turned to speak to Clare, Allie
was conscious of just how incredibly *flat* the other
woman was, and self-consciously crossed her arms
over her ample bosom, so blatantly displayed by her
low-cut blouse.

'Are you sure I can't help you with anything in

here?' Elaine was asking Clare.

'Not at all. Everything's under control. Just go out with Allie and relax on the terrace. I'll be able to join you in a couple of minutes,' Clare responded, and Allie sent her a curious look. Despite her friend's smile and pleasant manner, Allie could sense Clare's dislike of Elaine. It seemed odd, since Clare usually got on well with just about everyone. Besides, Elaine seemed too innocuous to arouse enmity in anyone. Why, she even got along well enough with that beast Linc Summerville to let him escort her to a party!

'As long as you're sure,' Elaine said charmingly. 'Perhaps I could slip this salad into the fridge until dinner, though.' She walked to the counter and started to open a large brown paper bag that was resting near the blender. 'I know you said we didn't need to bring anything, but I fixed a little something because it didn't seem right to come empty-handed.'

Tugging on the paper, Elaine exposed her 'little something'. It was a fruit salad, although that description didn't do justice to the work of art Elaine had prepared. Balls of melon, pineapple chunks and a myriad other exotic fruits resided in a hollowed-out half-shell of a water-melon. The edges were serrated and decorated with lemon slices. As Allie watched, Elaine reached back into the bag to withdraw several long sticks with squares of paper attached and placed them upright along the centre-line of the 'ship'.

'It's beautiful, Elaine,' Claire said stiffly. 'You shouldn't have gone to so much trouble.'

'It was nothing,' the other woman assured her airily. She went to the fridge and opened it to peer inside. 'Oh, dear, do you think there's going to be room in here for it?'

Clare joined Elaine in front of the open fridge

before she could start removing items, saying grimly, 'I'll clear a space.' Clare set about removing the salads and relish trays that she had prepared earlier and were crowding the interior of the refrigerator, and Elaine looked over to Allie.

'I think maybe I should go have a look at Linc's shirt. Greasy stains like that can be a real problem to get out, so the sooner it's dealt with, the better. I'd hate to think the shirt was ruined. Linc's not much of a bargain-hunter when it comes to buying clothes, and that shirt was brand new.'

She walked from the kitchen, leaving Allie overburdened with guilt. Maybe it hadn't been her fault that Linc's shirt had been covered in dressing, but she *had* been indirectly responsible. It certainly didn't help her conscience to find out it had been a new, expensive shirt.

When Clare had the refrigerator set to rights again, she took out a bottle of wine before slamming the door.

'Let's have a drink,' she suggested. 'After an encounter with Elaine, I always feel I need one.'

Allie hadn't been exactly comforted by the other woman's references to Linc's shirt; however, she couldn't understand Clare's animosity. As she accepted the glass of white wine from her friend, she asked, 'Don't you like her? She seems pleasant enough, and it was good of her to bring that salad. She must have gone to a lot of trouble.'

'That salad,' Clare said sourly, taking a large swallow of her wine and pulling a face. 'Everything I fixed is going to look like yesterday's leftovers now. The group we socialise with used to have a lot of pot-luck dinners, but after Elaine joined us we stopped. Most of us are pretty good cooks, but we don't have the time or energy to waste fussing in the kitchen. Every time we had one of those dinners, Elaine would show up with some work of art that made our efforts look like the dog's dinner. Maybe we're just vain, but we got awfully tired of being upstaged.' She lifted her glass again, drained it and set it aside. 'You'd be doing a real service to the women in my circle if you'd snaffle Linc away from her. We're all dreading the idea that he might go so far as to marry her and we'd be stuck with her for the rest of our lives!'

As Clare started cleaning up the splattered dressing from the counter-tops, Allie sipped her wine in silence. Take Linc away from Elaine? What a joke! Even if she wanted to, she wouldn't have a prayer. She glanced over to her friend. Of course, Clare didn't know about her first run-in with Linc. She had kept the details of that first meeting to herself, merely explaining that she had run out of petrol on the way to her friend's house. It had been too humiliating to recount.

She sighed as she put her wineglass aside and picked up a cloth to help Clare clean up. Her friend would find out soon enough that Elaine had a clear field with Linc as far as Allie came into it.

CHAPTER THREE

TWILIGHT was deepening into night when Allie slipped from the crowded living-room out on to the terrace. Most of Clare's guests had retreated inside at sunset, chased in by mosquitoes and the cooler night air. However, the house had seemed stuffy after a few minutes, prompting Allie to go back outside. She skirted the few groups of hardy souls that had lingered on the terrace, making for the far corner where the terrace wrapped around the side of the house.

Leaning against the railing, she stared out into the night, enjoying a moment of solitude. Playing the role of the dumb blonde for Clare's friends had been easy, mainly because she hadn't had to act. There hadn't been much choice but to murmur inane comments when she hadn't a clue about the subjects under discussion, she mused. She knew nothing about fishing or hockey or the price of strawberries. She rarely watched television, never read novels. Until tonight, she hadn't realised how narrow her interests were. When she'd worked at the Institute, conversation at the social gatherings she had attended had invariably centred on 'shop'—computers, mathematics, science. Even with Kevin, the talk had seldom strayed to less erudite topics.

She had enjoyed the evening, though. To her amazement, Clare's scheme seemed actually to be working. While Allie had never been exactly a wallflower at gatherings, people had tended to treat her with a certain deference, a certain reserve. It was almost as if they were a little afraid of her, intimidated by her noted intelligence.

Tonight, though, she felt she had been accepted wholeheartedly by Clare's friends, by the women as well as the men. Several of them had suggested future meetings for lunch or shopping. As for the single men in the group—a tiny smile tugged Allie's lips. Her ego was purring like a well-fed cat. She'd never been treated to that kind of attention before, fussed over, catered to. She wouldn't have been female if she hadn't lapped it up. It had even taken a bit of strategy just to slip away alone for a breath of fresh air. She could have had her pick of escorts.

At that moment, Allie felt a strange prickling sensation along the back of her neck. Perhaps she hadn't managed to evade her suitors for a few moments, after all. Slowly she turned to look behind her. Unnoticed by her, Linc Summerville had also come outside and was now leaning against the corner of the house, watching her. His scrutiny was unnerving, and Allie eyed him cautiously. *He* hadn't been one of the circle of admirers that had surrounded her most of the evening, although she supposed she couldn't blame him. His two previous encounters with her had proved inauspicious, to say the least.

Why had he joined her now? Glancing along the terrace she saw that the others had all gone inside.

'It's cool out here,' Allie said, like a coward, rubbing her hands over the goose-bumps that had sprung up on her arms. The breeze hadn't bothered her before, but she hadn't known that she was alone with Linc then. 'I think I'll go back inside.'

She took a step away from the railing at the same time that Linc straightened and moved towards her.

'I wanted to talk to you for a moment.'

Even though there was a good foot between them when he stopped, Allie still had to steal herself not to retreat back to the railing. She fixed her eyes on his shirt, then hastily raised her gaze to somewhere in the vicinity of his chin. It was a curious phenomenon. Greg's shirt was too small for Linc, and the material stretched taut over the rock-hard muscles of his chest. It made her incredibly aware of his male strength and power. She wasn't normally susceptible to the magnetic draw of the opposite sex. Her physical relationship with Kevin had been perfunctory and amazingly passionless. She'd only wanted it because it had seemed that they should have something more between them than the common ground of mere business colleagues. Even with the sex, though, that was all she'd really ever had with Kevin, she thought unhappily.

Linc said suddenly, intruding into her thoughts, 'You look different tonight from the way you did the other day.'

Allie gave him a puzzled glance, sensing that that wasn't what he'd sought her out to say. 'Do I?' She shrugged with apparent nonchalance. 'Maybe it's because I'm not soaking wet.' Even if she hadn't been caught in the rain that day, she knew she would have looked different. She didn't want to admit it to him, though. Although she'd been delighted with her new look, in retrospect, there seemed something appallingly vain in having spent that much time and effort on her appearance.

'Perhaps that's it,' he said, pensively. Linc lifted his hand and fingered one of the locks of golden hair that framed her face. 'I rather liked that ''lost kitten in the rain'' look you had that day, though,' he murmured, half to himself.

'Oh,' Allie said uncertainly. The back of his hand accidentally brushed against her cheek and she started in reaction. Immediately, he withdrew his hand, letting it fall to his side. Allie felt a stab of disappointment. Glancing upwards to the clear night sky, black velvet studded with diamond stars, she had an unreasoning wish for a sudden cloudburst.

She half turned away from him, staring out across the Strait. The moon was rising above the horizon, bathing the ocean in pale silver light. It was a beautiful, romantic evening, and she was alone out here on the terrace with Linc. She could sense his nearness, smell the faint tang of the spicy aftershave he was wearing.

She wondered again why he had joined her. She'd made such an awful first impression on him that she'd have thought he would go to great lengths to avoid her. She slid him a brief glance, her pulse quickening. Was it possible that, despite everything, he was attracted to her? He'd called her beautiful that first day. His comment just now seemed to reaffirm that opinion. He'd touched her hair. She was cautious since her experience with Kevin, but the novelty of the present situation intrigued her. Men didn't usually seek out Dr Smith to make a pass at her. If he were to kiss her, how would she react?

'Clare mentioned that you were planning to spend the summer here—find a place to rent in the area.'

Allie looked back at him and saw he had moved, increasing the space between them. The moon had risen over the horizon, and by its pale light she searched his expression. She must have been imagining things. He didn't appear to be contemplating kissing anyone. She sighed, then answered him. 'That's right.'

'The thing is, I have a cabin on my property. Clare knows I've been thinking of finding a tenant for it. She's sure to mention it to you.'

Was he offering to rent it to her? 'What's it like?' she asked curiously.

'It's nothing fancy,' he said quickly. 'Just a couple of rooms. It was on the property when I bought it, and I stayed in it when I was having my present house built. It's quite primitive, actually.'

He wasn't much of a salesman, Allie thought. There was something faintly off-putting in his sketchy description of the cabin. On the other hand, perhaps he was just being frank. She was about to tell him that she'd like to look at it none the less, but he spoke first.

'I don't really think that it would suit you. I just thought that I'd warn you that Clare will probably want to drag you over to have a look at it, but you might as well save yourself the effort.'

'Oh,' Allie said, disconcerted. 'Surely it wouldn't hurt for me to at least see it? I mean, after all, if Clare thinks . . .'

'But I'm telling you, you wouldn't be comfortable in it,' Linc cut in. 'Besides, I'm not sure that I still want to rent it out.'

Allie didn't have a high IQ for nothing. She frosted her voice with ice so he wouldn't be able to detect her hurt at his snub. 'Don't you mean, you don't want to rent it to me?'

He hesitated for several moments. She wished that it wasn't so dark out here on the terrace, so she could tell if he had the grace to blush.

At last he said baldly, 'You're brighter than I gave you credit for.'

Linc Summerville had probably never blushed in

his life, Allie thought angrily.

'It's nothing personal,' he went on to say. 'The thing is, I spend a lot of time in Vancouver, my business is over there. I have a housekeeper who looks after my son for me while I'm away, but I wanted someone in the cabin whom she could fall back on in an emergency, someone she could count on.'

'And she couldn't count on me?'

Ignoring her interjection, he went on, 'Mrs Dorcus does a great job, but she's a little temperamental. She doesn't suffer fools gladly, and it would be better to have someone in the cabin who would pretty much keep to themselves.'

'Meaning that I am a fool,' Allie said acidly. 'I'm overwhelmed by your flattery.' She half stepped forward to go past him and back into the house. However, he caught her by the upper arms and held her facing him.

'I'm putting this badly and I'm sorry. I'm not trying to offend you.'

'You're doing a good job of it, though!'

She heard his sigh. He was still holding her by the arms, his hands creating burning patches of heat on her cool flesh. They also sparked an unwanted awareness kindling in the base of her stomach. Allie made a little movement to cause him to release her. He didn't, but spoke instead.

'Look, you're a very attractive, very sexy lady with a lot of good qualities, I'm sure,' he said gently. 'Unfortunately, I need someone who's self-sufficient to take over the cabin.'

'And what would you know about my self-sufficiency?' she demanded, although she didn't know why she was arguing. She wouldn't live on his property now if he offered her Buckingham Palace. She wasn't even sure she wanted to live in the same province!

'I don't think I should bring that up,' he responded drily. Allie felt colour moving up her cheeks, and she pressed her lips together in angry embarrassment. You'd think no one had ever run out of petrol before! 'Some women need a lot of looking after,' he continued. 'There's nothing wrong with that, and I'm sure that practically every man at this party tonight would be more than happy to take on the job. I simply don't have time, though. I can't be running around after you, and that's what I would end up having to do if you took that cabin. You're the type who'd always be losing your key or needing help to get your car started in the morning. I don't have room in my life to take on a clinging vine.'

'I didn't ask you to,' Allie said in a tight voice. The trouble was, he wasn't that far out in his assessment of her. She never had managed to deal efficiently with the trivial, mundane parts of life. The couple who ran the apartment building where she lived had frequently been called on to help her out. 'I didn't ask you to,' she repeated, her voice shaking as she tried to control an unexpected desire to cry. Why should she care what he thought of her?

She did, however. Pulling free of his hold, she turned her back to him and gripped the railing to stare blindly out into the night.

Behind her, Linc swore softly. 'I'm sorry. I was just trying to explain my position. I know I was blunt, but I didn't want to hurt your feelings.' When she didn't answer, he asked worriedly, 'You're not crying, are you?'

Allie felt his hand touch her shoulder uncertainly and hastily tried to blink away the moisture that filmed her eyes. There was an enormous lump blocking her throat, and she couldn't seem to swallow it away so that she could speak without betraying herself.

Linc muttered another imprecation and then he was turning her to face him. At that moment, someone switched on the outside light and Allie knew he'd caught the sheen of moisture on her lashes. Quickly she jerked free, twisting away so he could no longer see her face.

'So this is where you two have hidden yourselves,' Clare said, walking along the terrace to join them. When she reached them, she asked, 'What are you up to—or shouldn't I ask?'

If she only knew! Allie would hardly call these past few minutes with that insulting beast a dalliance. Surreptitiously Allie rubbed the tears from her eyes with the base of her palms before turning to greet her friend. She needn't have bothered about Clare seeing the tears, for, surprisingly, Linc had moved to position himself so that she was sheltered by his shadow. He cast her a quick look before saying to Clare, 'We were just discussing that cabin on my property. It looks as if Allie's going to rent it from me.'

Clare's exclamation of pleasure drowned out Allie's gasp. She stared at Linc, bewildered by his abrupt about-face, while Clare prattled on, 'This is super! Linc's place is only a couple of miles down the road, so you won't be far away. First thing tomorrow, we can start getting you organised for moving you in. I've got lots of extra dishes and stuff you can use, so you shouldn't have to buy much. Let's see . . .'

'Clare?' Greg was standing in the doorway of the house. 'You out there?'

'You need something? I'll be right there,' she called

to him.

'Go ahead, Clare,' Linc suggested. 'We'll be right along.'

As soon as the other woman had departed, he turned to Allie. Before he could speak, though, she got in first.

'What made you change your mind?'

He stayed silent for several moments, then suddenly lifted his hand to rub long fingers over the nape of his neck. 'Just don't be more of a bloody nuisance than you have to be.'

Allie glared at him in irritation as he started to turn away, exploding with, 'I suppose it never occurred to you that I might not want to rent your precious cabin? That I'm no more keen to have you for a landlord than you are to have me for a tenant!'

There was a faint gleam of malice in his navy eyes as he looked at her. 'Well, then, I'll let you tell Clare,' he said mildly.

With a snort of annoyance, Allie moved to push past him and go inside. Clare was already carried away by the idea. Unless the place was an absolute hovel, her friend would never accept that Allie didn't want to live in Linc Summerville's cabin.

She had only gone a couple of paces when Linc caught her arm and halted her. He had a habit of doing that. 'Allie,' he said, holding out something to her. She looked down and saw his white handkerchief. 'Your mascara's run under your eyes. You look like a raccoon,' he gibed. 'Maybe you should wipe it off before you go in.'

Pushing the handkerchief into her hand, he walked away. In the brief seconds before he did so, his lips had brushed her cheek. As she stared after him in bewildered anger, Allie slowly began to repair the damages.

As Allie didn't *really* want to move into Linc
Summerville's cabin, it was rather disconcerting to
discover that was exactly what she was doing three
weeks later. Clare and Greg were expecting an influx
of house-guests, so it wasn't convenient for them to
continue having her. However, there were plenty of
places to rent, and Allie could have made Clare
understand her reluctance to live on Linc's property.

She couldn't quite figure out why she hadn't made
more of an effort. Even if Clare wouldn't have
understood, Allie was long past the stage of being
bullied. Since leaving university at seventeen, she had
taken full charge of her life. Up until that time, her
parents had mapped out her existence, selecting the
courses she took in school, enrolling her in specialised
mathematics and computer camps during her breaks.
However, when they decided that she should accept a
teaching position with a major university back east
following her graduation, Allie had rebelled. She was
far more interested in research than in teaching, so the
job offered her by the Institute was more attractive
and suitable. However, while the Institute was highly
respected among scientists, it was virtually unheard of
by the general public. Having a daughter working
there would carry none of the prestige among the
Smiths' friends that a position at the well-known
university would have.

The schism that resulted from Allie's making her
own career choice had never healed. At first, her
parents had promoted the rift, wanting to punish her
for her disobedience. However, as she began making a
name for herself, and occasionally receiving a mention
in the Press, they had made overtures to bring her

back into the fold. By that time, though, Allie understood their motivations much better than she had as a child, and kept her distance, seeing them only infrequently. They placed her in the same category as their Cadillac and classically elegant home with the swimming pool in the back yard. A highly educated, super-intelligent child was a status symbol, and Allie never wanted to go back to being the prime exhibit at their cocktail parties, paraded before the guests like a trained monkey.

Her parents wouldn't approve of her present situation, Allie mused as she drew her car to a halt in front of Linc's cabin. They hadn't been pleased with her when she was working at the Institute and living in a comfortable apartment. Now, not only was she unemployed and living off her savings, but her summer accommodation was every bit as primitive as Linc had warned her.

Although it did boast indoor plumbing, Allie had to admit that it was nevertheless pretty rustic when she'd viewed it with Clare a few days after the party. Built on an A-frame design, the lower floor consisted of an L-shaped sitting-room/kitchen, a minuscule bedroom that would barely accommodate a single bed, and a tiny bathroom. The narrow kitchen area was separated from the sitting-room by a wooden counter skirted with faded calico. The floors were bare plywood, the ceilings merely clear plastic sheeting over the fibreglass insulation between the joists. The unfinished upper floor formed by an open loft over the kitchen and bedroom below was reached by a crude, home-made ladder.

On the other hand, it might not be too bad once there was some furniture and maybe a few rugs, Allie told herself as she left the car and moved towards the front door. She turned her back to it for a moment to look out over the scene before her. The cabin was sited on a bluff rising above the rocky shore that afforded a fabulous view of sea and islands. The air was fresh and clear as crystal, the sky a rich robin's egg blue. Allie sighed faintly with pleasure. Whatever the drawbacks of the cabin itself, its surroundings were a paradise.

When she turned back towards the house, the door was open and Linc Summerville was leaning against the jamb, watching her.

Allie jumped slightly. 'You startled me!'

'Sorry,' he said, although he didn't look particularly apologetic. 'The kitchen tap was dripping, so I came over to change the washer on it so that it would be fixed before you moved in.'

'I see.' Instead of gratitude, Allie felt a niggling sense of irritation. Her act of playing the dumb blonde had succeeded only too well with Linc, and it annoyed her that he didn't even credit her with the intelligence to install a simple washer. She didn't understand it. She wasn't even interested in Linc Summerville. She didn't *need* to be. Since Clare's party, she had had several dates with different men that she'd met there. While none of them had any idea of the extent of her intelligence, neither had they treated her as though she were exceptionally stupid. Only Linc seemed to think that—and he hadn't shown any interest in seeing her socially.

He had moved from his casual position in the doorway, and was looking past her shoulder to her packed car. 'So you're all ready to move in today.'

Allie nodded, automatically shifting so that she could follow his gaze. She could see the boxes and bags jammed nearly to the roof in the back seat.

Harold was among them, carefully packed in a padded
carton. Harold was a very special fellow who, in a fit
of whimsy, Allie had named after 'Hal', the computer
in 2001. He was a Compaq with a 640k memory, and
she'd added a 2-meg. above-board memory and hard
disk drive as well as an 8087 maths co-processor. She
almost wished that she could show him to Linc. He
knew about computers. Clare had told her that he
owned a computer software development firm in
Vancouver. He wouldn't think she was so stupid once
he saw her putting Harold through his paces.

But he would never have the opportunity. She
turned back to look at him. 'I brought most of my
things over. Clare's coming along in her station-
wagon later with some dishes and bedding she
rounded up for me.'

'Fine. She passed my message on that you didn't
need to worry about getting any furniture, didn't she?
I told her I would take care of the basics.'

'Yes, she told me.' Allie had wondered about that.
Linc had made it more than clear that he didn't want
her causing him any bother, but he had offered to
furnish the cabin for her. She guessed that it couldn't
be that much trouble to go down to the local junk
shop and pick up some second-hand furniture.

'You haven't seen it since we started fixing it up,
have you?' he commented and stepped back so that
she could precede him into the cabin. 'Come have a
look and see what you think.'

Allie only took a few paces into the cabin before
shock halted her. The interior was almost
unrecognisable from her previous visit. It even
smelled different. The dank, musky odour she had
noticed before was replaced by the clean, 'new' smell
of carpeting, paint and sawdust. The walls and

ceilings had been finished and colour-washed in off-white, and soft dove-grey carpeting covered the previously bare floor. As for the old furniture she had been expecting . . . there was a suspiciously new-looking sofa in dusky rose and a pair of wing chairs patterned with flowers in the same colour. Polished mahogany end-tables were scattered about the room, holding up bright brass table-lamps.

Allie looked over to Linc, feeling dazed. It was incredible to think that he had done all this for her. Maybe he didn't dislike her as much as she thought. Maybe now she could admit to herself that she didn't dislike him either.

Allie moistened her lips. 'I . . . er . . . I don't know what to say. It's lovely. You must have gone . . .'

'It's no big deal,' he cut her off, shrugging in irritation. He seemed embarrassed and discomfited by her gratitude. 'The place needed to be fixed up before it was let, anyway. It'll be easier to find someone else to take it over after you leave if I have it furnished.'

Allie bit her lip as she watched him walk away from her towards the kitchen. Of course, he hadn't done all this just for her. It was rather foolish of her to think that he might have. Still . . . her eyes rested on the spot where the crude wooden counter had stood. It had been torn out and replaced by modern oak cabinets topped with formica. Beyond it, she could see that the entire kitchen had been remodelled. He had gone to so much trouble!

'I still want to thank you. It wouldn't have bothered me to live in it the way it was, but this is really fantastic!'

He gave her a look of faint exasperation, then said drily, 'Well, I'm glad you like it. Come look over the rest of it,' he suggested, beckoning her into the kitchen.

Even though she knew she was annoying him, Allie couldn't prevent little murmurs of appreciation escaping as they toured the rest of the house. The kitchen was a dream, compact but convenient, with gleaming counter-tops and appliances. The bathroom had been completely refitted with ivory fixtures and a modern shower-cabinet.

By the time they reached the bedroom, Linc was looking quite put-out with her. Allie's eyes lit up when she saw the exquisite broderie anglaise quilt gracing the divan bed and the matching curtains at the window. She turned to Linc, her mouth opening to comment, but he spoke first.

'I know, it's gorgeous,' he said sardonically.

Allie blushed, coming down to earth with a thud as she caught his mocking expression. Now she was the one who was embarrassed. It was one thing to show appreciation, but she'd been spewing out praise for half an hour, rendering it meaningless. 'I'm sorry I got carried away. It's just that everything is so . . .' She shrugged, unable to complete the sentence.

'You finally ran out of adjectives,' Linc said with mock relief.

Avoiding his eyes, Allie looked away and her gaze fell on to the bed. A tiny shiver rippled down her spine as she looked at it, imagining . . . She hadn't even thought about their being alone together in the bedroom until that moment.

Suddenly, she was uncomfortable. The saliva left her mouth and she swallowed hard.

When she looked back over to Linc, he was eyeing her consideringly, a faint gleam lighting his navy eyes. She had a feeling he knew exactly what she had been thinking. He said, 'There is a better way of showing me how much you like what I've had done to the cabin than just telling me.'

Deliberately obtuse, Allie gave him a puzzled look, frowning slightly as he moved to stand directly in front of her. Of course, he was only joking.

'A better way,' he reiterated. His hands moved to her shoulders before she had a chance to move away, and he tugged her forwards. 'A much, much better way,' he murmured as his head lowered and his mouth covered hers.

CHAPTER FOUR

FOR A moment Allie stood perfectly still within Linc's arms, uncertain what to do. Had his kiss been forceful, demanding, she would have bolted, wrenching from his embrace and probably kicking him in the shins for good measure. But it wasn't like that. His mouth was cool and passionless over hers, his embrace steady and almost impersonal. It was a friendly, perfunctory kiss, nothing more. It was a silly game he was playing with her.

Knowing that, despite that, she felt a tantalising warmth slowly begin to trickle through her, thawing her inhibitions. She had been kissed before, with passion, with desire, and yet those kisses had never sparked this slow, burning urgency that she was feeling now.

As the heat built within her, Allie relaxed against him, moving her body closer to his as her arms lifted to encircle his neck. Her lips parted to invite his pillage, and she sensed his hesitation, as though he might at any moment withdraw. Her arms tightened unconsciously, holding him to her as she moved against him, thigh against thigh, her breasts flattening against his chest. Suddenly it was the most important thing in the world that he should not release her, cast her from him. In a deep, elemental part of her, she felt she might die from the blow if he did.

She felt his shudder, the low groan somewhere deep within his throat, and knew that he would not leave her. The hands that had been on her shoulders stroked down her back to her waist, confident and firm as they drew her closer. His lips searched hers, his tongue probing the softness of her inner lips. Melting in his embrace, Allie's hands caressed his shoulders, her fingertips delighting in the hard strength of him.

Easing a space between them, Linc slipped his hand over her throbbing breast and kneaded the swollen globe. A dart of pure ecstasy shot through Allie, liquefying her bones so that she was forced to cling to him. His mouth trailed a path of flames along her cheek to her jaw, then down her throat. He moved his hand to release the top button of her blouse, his fingertips brushing the smooth satin of her skin. At the same time, he turned her, gently easing her towards the bed.

'Allie!'

Like children playing statues, they froze at the sound of Clare's voice coming from the living-room.

'Allie! Where are you?'

At the second call, Allie pushed herself free of Linc's arms and stood staring at him with wide, appalled eyes. 'Oh!' she whispered, the reality of the situation crashing in on her. She'd been a hair's breadth from going to bed with Linc. If Clare's voice hadn't interrupted . . .

Linc's eyes held hers, but he also looked shaken. Then Allie saw him take a deep breath, and a mask seemed to drop over his features, leaving them expressionless. 'We're in here,' he called out in a steady voice. 'I was just showing Allie around.'

As he stepped around her towards the door, he said in a harsh undertone, 'Straighten your clothes.'

Allie's hand went to the front of her blouse. The top

buttons were open, exposing the swell of her breasts, inadequately concealed by the fragile lace of her bra. Fingers shaking, she clumsily did up the buttons, aware of Linc waiting for her by the door.

At last the task was finished, and she looked over to him. Although his features were still impassive, she could sense anger simmering within him. 'Linc?' she questioned timidly, seeking reassurance.

His gaze slowly drifted down her form, then beyond her to the bed. Finally he met her eyes. There was no masking the contempt in his dark blue eyes now. 'Are you ready to go?'

'You started it,' Allie accused, ignoring his question. '*You* kissed me.' Anger raised her chin to a proud angle, but inside she felt sick with humiliation.

Linc shrugged. 'I did it as a joke. Too bad Clare showed up. We were just getting to the punch-line.' He smiled, and the set of his lips was cruel.

Allie paled, her grey eyes stricken. He couldn't have hurt her more if he had slapped her. Linc's smile faded on seeing her expression, the harsh set of his features fading. He took a step forward, holding his hand out to her. 'I'm sorry. That was uncalled for.'

'Go to hell,' Allie rasped, pushing past him to reach the door.

When Allie left the bedroom, she found Clare in the sitting-room. Fortunately, the older woman was too engrossed in admiring the redecoration of the cabin to notice Allie's somewhat *distraite* air. By the time it came for them to unload the bits and pieces of domestic paraphernalia loaded into Clare's station-wagon, Allie had regained her composure. She was helped considerably in this by Linc's departure. He was too much of a gentleman not to offer to help with the unpacking, but he accepted Allie's refusal of his help without argument. She suspected he didn't want to be around her any more than she wanted to be in his company.

Clare left as soon as her car was unloaded. Her next batch of house-guests was arriving that day, and she had to meet them at Departure Bay in Nanaimo where the ferry from Vancouver docked. Leaving the boxes of dishes, cooking utensils, bedding, etcetera stacked in the centre of the kitchen floor, Allie worked to get her own car unloaded. She only had a couple of suitcases for her clothes, but there were numerous boxes of books, papers, computer disks, and, of course, Harold, which needed to be unloaded.

The crude ladder to the loft had been replaced by a narrow staircase of wrought iron with wooden steps, and Allie decided to use the upper floor as an office. Linc hadn't furnished it, probably assuming she had no use for the space, but it was carpeted and freshly painted. Once she got a desk and chair, it would make an ideal work area—besides, she wasn't as enamoured with the downstairs as she had been when she'd first seen it.

It was rather silly, actually, but she couldn't control her feelings. When they'd come out of the bedroom, Linc had stayed for a few minutes talking to Clare. Naturally, the other woman's comments had centred on the transformation of the cabin. It was then that Linc had mentioned that Elaine had had a hand in choosing the decorations.

It shouldn't have made a difference, but it was after hearing Linc tell Clare that, that Allie began having second thoughts about the cabin's interior. Of course, Elaine's role in the proceedings probably had nothing to do with it. She certainly wasn't *jealous* of the other woman. How could she be? Allie didn't even like Linc, so the woman was welcome to him. It was probably just that, after the initial surprise had worn off, she'd had a better chance to assess the changes. Grey and rose for the living-room seemed muted and a bit bland once she thought about it. As for the broderie anglaise in the bedroom, it gave the room an aura of sickly-sweet femininity that might be cute in a little girl's sanctum, but was hardly suitable for a grown woman.

Once she had carried everything upstairs to the loft, Allie spent a few minutes unpacking Harold, then decided to do a brief systems check on him. He'd been stowed away in his crate since she'd left the Institute, and she wanted to be sure that he hadn't sustained any damage during her trip out to the coast.

It was a mistake. Once she'd seated herself cross-legged on the floor in front of the computer screen, Allie was lost to the real world. The hours of the day melted away, and it wasn't until her stomach rumbled persistently that she returned to the realities of life. She'd forgotten all about lunch, and it was almost time for the evening meal.

Downstairs, the kitchen looked as if a cardboard box factory had exploded in it. All the cartons that she and Clare had unloaded from her friend's car were strewn around exactly where they had dumped them. Allie grimaced at the chaos, then did a futile check of the empty cupboards and fridge. She'd forgotten all about buying groceries.

'Whatya doin'?'

Startled by the voice, Allie jumped, knocking several wads of crumpled newspaper packing from the carton she'd been rummaging through and on to the floor. Turning towards the sound, she saw a small boy staring at her. The back door of the cabin, which had been closed, was standing wide open, and as she watched the boy stepped through and into the kitchen.

He studied her for several moments with undisguised curiosity, then looked around the kitchen. He wrinkled his nose. After being shut up all day, the cabin smelt strongly of the new carpeting, although it wasn't a particularly objectionable odour. However, the boy said, 'It smells yukky in here.' He kicked at a newspaper wad lying at his feet and sent it scudding across the floor to rest under the kitchen table.

In general, Allie liked children, although she'd never had much to do with them. However, all things considered, this one seemed to be a rather rude little boy, Allie assessed. Hadn't he ever heard of knocking? He wasn't exactly ready to go visiting, either. Dressed in a grubby T-shirt and short trousers, his face was streaked with dirt, his untidy mop of dark hair crying out for a good brush.

Before she could suggest he leave, though, he repeated his question. 'Whatya doin'?'

'I'm looking for something to eat,' Allie admitted curtly. 'Maybe you ought to go on home and let me get on with it.'

He ignored her suggestion, coming forward to peer into the box she had been ransacking. He then moved over to the refrigerator, and without invitation pulled open its door and peered into its bare interior. As he turned back to Allie, he slammed the door shut behind him. 'How come you don't keep your food in the 'frigerator like we do?'

Allie really wondered why she felt compelled to offer any explanations to him, but she found herself saying, 'I do normally, there and in the cupboard. But I haven't had time to go shopping yet. I was looking in there to see if my friend might have slipped in a packet of cookies when she packed the carton.'

He looked up at her, his dark eyes lighting up. 'I like cookies.'

Allie's mouth twitched. He was a pushy little twerp, but there was something appealing about him. 'Do you?' she replied drily.

'I like cookies real good.' He looked down at the carton, his gaze lingering as though he were contemplating a treasure chest filled with jewels. He raised his eyes back to her. 'I'm a real good cookie-finder. I found the cookies even when Mrs Dorcus hid them way, way up in the back of the cupboard over the 'frigerator.'

Suddenly, the boy delved into the carton, chucking out the newspaper with gay abandon and endangering the glasses and dinnerware that it had been protecting.

'Jason! Just what do you think you're doing?'

Allie turned and saw Linc Summerville standing in the doorway. That morning, she had felt that if she never saw him again it would be too soon. Right now, though, she viewed his appearance as a godsend. She hadn't a clue as to how she was supposed to handle this little monster that had invaded her kitchen.

The little monster looked up and regarded the newcomer unconcernedly. 'Hi, Dad,' he greeted Linc nonchalantly before burrowing back into the box, nearly tipping over into it headfirst.

While Allie digested the knowledge that this brat was Linc's son, he strode across the room and pulled the child out of the box by the waistband of his shorts. Setting the child on his feet, he looked down at him. There was a steely glint in Linc's eyes and a tight set to his mouth that didn't bode well for his son. 'I asked you what you were doing over here. I told you to stay in the yard and play until supper was ready.'

Unimpressed by his father's obvious wrath, Jason answered easily, 'I was looking for this lady's cookies.' He made a movement as though to return to his search, but Linc's hard hands on his shoulders held him where he was.

Linc frowned slightly, glancing over to Allie. She didn't have an opportunity to explain before Jason pre-empted her. 'She said they were in this box, but I think she was lying. I couldn't find them and I looked and looked.' He kicked the box disgustedly with the toe of his shoe, causing the crockery inside to rattle ominously. 'You know, she doesn't have *anything* at all in her 'frigerator?' he told his father in an appalled tone. 'She said she had cookies, but I couldn't find them!'

Linc gave her an odd look and Allie averted her face. She wondered if Linc would even recognise her if her cheeks weren't beet-red. She'd never been a blusher, but since meeting him she seemed to do little else. The man had an absolute talent for catching her in embarrassing situations.

'I didn't have time to go shopping,' she finally mumbled when the lengthening silence became unbearable.

'I see,' Linc said. His gaze swept over the chaotic room. She could read his thoughts. It was only too obvious that she hadn't spent her time unpacking. With dread, she waited for him to ask her just exactly what she *had* been doing all day—frantically wondering how she would answer. However, the question never came, as Jason lunged back into the conversation.

'I'm hungry. Is supper ready yet?'

'It is,' Linc said grimly, turning his attention back
to his son. 'Maybe you should be sent to bed without
it, though. I told you to stay around the house and not
come over here bothering Miss Smith. You disobeyed
me, and you're going to have to be punished.'

'Ah, Dad,' Jason wailed. 'I'll *starve* if you don't let
me have supper.' He clutched his stomach and
groaned dramatically. 'Without any food I'll be
deaded and . . . and . . . you'll have to bury me and put
flowers on my grave.' With his arms still wrapped
about his stomach, he gave another pathetic groan and
stared up mutely at his father's stern countenance.
'Please, Daddy, I don't want to be deaded like
Mommy.' A single sad tear trailed slowly down the
babyish curve of his cheek. 'I miss my mommy.'
Wresting free of his father's hold, he flung himself at
Allie, burying his head in her mid-section and sobbing
pitifully.

It was a scene that would melt a heart of stone, but
when Allie looked over to Linc she saw his expression
had grown even harder, his jaw clenched in silent
anger, his eyes glacier-cold.

He walked over to the boy and firmly disengaged
his arms from around Allie. Holding him before him,
he said sternly, 'Jason, I want you to get home right
now. I'll expect you to be bathed, in your pyjamas and
in bed by the time I get there. Do you understand?'

The child's eyes were pools of anguish, his little boy
mouth quivering with hurt. 'Yes, Dad,' Jason
muttered. Head bent, he shuffled obediently out of
the door.

Allie stared after the child in amazement. She had
harboured no great opinion of Linc Summerville
before, but she had never imagined that he . . . that

anyone . . . could be so utterly cruel and heartless to a poor, defenceless, *motherless* child. Why, he was a monster!

And, as if that heartbreaking little scene had never occurred, Linc said matter-of-factly, 'Since you haven't had a chance to get in any foodstuff, you can have dinner with me. Mrs Dorcus always makes plenty.'

Allie gaped at him. 'I don't . . . couldn't eat with you—you—*sadist*! I'd choke. What do you do for recreation . . . pull the wings off flies?' She whirled around and stared mutely down at the floor. Her hands were trembling and she laced them in front of her to still their movement. She'd been appallingly rude. His face had told her that. But he deserved it.

Heavy silence lay over the kitchen, broken only by the dull throbbing of her pulse in her ears. Finally she heard Linc turn away, and she released the breath she had been unconsciously holding.

Linc didn't leave, though. Although he moved a few paces towards the door, he stopped and turned back to her. 'I don't really owe you any explanations, but if you're going to be around here all summer you'll undoubtedly be coming into contact with my son occasionally. You'd better understand that he does a lot of things purely for effect.'

She didn't want to hear his excuses; there was no excuse for him.

When she didn't react, Linc snapped, 'For Pete's sake, turn around. I have no intention of standing here carrying on a conversation with your back!'

Although she had had no intention of accommodating him, she found herself turning to face him. 'Jason wasn't carrying on for effect! His grief was very real.'

Linc treated her to a look of exasperation. 'It wasn't.'

'Clare told me that you were a widower. Are you denying that Jason's mother is dead?'

'I'm not denying it,' he said heavily. 'But Natalie has nothing to do with that little scene. That was pure television.'

'What are you talking about?'

'Jason's mother died when he was two. That was nearly five years ago. When a child loses a parent at that age, that long ago, he or she retains very little memory of them. It's just a sad fact of life, and Jason is no exception. He isn't hurting for his mother; he doesn't even remember her. Even *I* seldom think of her any more.' Allie gave him a keen glance. While he might be a harassed parent, he didn't really look like a grieving widower. For no reason at all, she felt a sudden relaxation of tension.

Linc continued, 'Jason has, however, quite recently discovered the emotional appeal of being a "poor motherless little boy". His heartbreaking little speech was quite frankly lifted almost word for word from a programme he recently saw on television. He saw it over at one of his friend's houses. Unfortunately, the boy's mother inadvertently drew his attention to the parallel between the character on the programme, who had lost his mother, albeit at an older age and much more recently, and himself. I believe he managed to coax an extra dessert out of her by playing it up. Since then, he has tried it out on just about every new person he meets.'

Allie regarded him uncertainly. His explanation did seem plausible; she didn't even know why she was wavering. It wasn't as though she'd even liked the little boy when he had been here. And yet . . . 'Are you really sending him to bed without supper?'

'It's what he deserves for flaunting my instructions, but . . .' Linc shrugged. 'I'm afraid my housekeeper would never allow it. She'll fix him something on a tray, probably his favourite dishes, and give it to him in his room whatever I say. Jason has Mrs Dorcus firmly wrapped around his little finger.'

'I see.' She didn't know quite what else to say beyond that. Suddenly she felt incredibly awkward in his presence. Distractedly, she reached down and picked up one of the newspaper balls littering the floor, and slowly began smoothing the wrinkles from it.

'And what about your supper?' Linc asked.

'My supper?'

'I invited you to have dinner with me, remember?'

'Oh . . . oh, yes, of course.'

'Will you come?'

Allie gave him an unsure look. One part of her very desperately wanted to share the meal with him, and it had nothing to do with the pangs of hunger assaulting her stomach. It made no sense, though. She felt awkward and ill at ease in his company. Besides, she didn't want a repeat of that scene this morning.

She sent him a surreptitious glance from beneath her lashes. She *didn't* want him kissing her like that again, did she?

'This place is a mess. I should stay here and clean it up.'

'It won't run away, and you still need to eat. You haven't any food in the house . . . my sons tells me not even cookies.' The skin at the corners of his eyes crinkled as he smiled at her.

'That's true,' Allie admitted. However, there were a couple of small grocery stores in the Cedar area. It

would only take a few minutes in the car to get to one
and pick up some supplies. A quick bowl of soup and
she could get down to putting all this stuff away.

She was going to explain all that to him, but the
words dried on her lips as she saw his expression of
gentle coaxing. 'Come have dinner with me, Allie,' he
ordered softly.

'I'd have to change.'

'I'll wait for you,' Linc said easily.

She smiled suddenly. 'It won't take me long to get
ready.'

Linc's home was nestled at the base of the bluff on
which the cabin was sited. A steep pathway led
through the trees, linking the two dwellings. As Allie
gingerly negotiated her way down it, she wondered if
changing into a full-skirted sundress and pumps was
such a good idea. It was one of the outfits Clare had
helped her buy, feminine and a little sexy. Why she
was wasting her 'man-bait' on Linc was a mystery. He
already had a girlfriend and, even if he hadn't had,
he'd only kissed her for a joke. Besides, it looked as if
it was going to be a toss-up as to whether her dress
would be torn to shreds by the blackberry brambles
before or after she broke her ankle on the rock-strewn
path.

When Linc clasped her hand to help her negotiate
the uneven footing, though, she forgot all about what
she was wearing. Something about his warm touch
addled her brain, driving all other thoughts and
sensations from her head. Even after he released her
hand at the foot of the path, she was slow to recover
her wits. She only received the barest impression of
the outside of his house, a modern cedar and glass
edifice, before he led her inside.

In the foyer he said, 'Wait for me in the living-room while I let Mrs Dorcus know that I've brought you back for dinner.' He gestured to the archway behind Allie.

'Sure,' Allie agreed, watching him go down the hall that led off in the opposite direction before turning to enter the sitting-room.

It was dominated by the view from the wide window-wall on the ocean side of the house. There was a panoramic seascape of water and islands gleaming in the early evening sunlight. Although it beckoned to her, Allie resisted the temptation to savour the view. It matched that from the cabin, only from a slightly different aspect. She was frankly more interested in inspecting Linc's living-room, looking for clues to his personality.

The room had an air of rustic elegance with a masculine flavour. Western red cedar panelled the walls, the warm richness of the wood carried through in the luxurious gold plush carpeting. A long sofa, covered in buttery soft leather, faced the natural stone fireplace at the far end of the room. Occasional chairs and tables were scattered about in cosy, conversational groups. Allie was immediately drawn to the chess-board set up on a low table in front of the fireplace. One set of men were carved from dark green jade, the other from pale green milky jade. The squares of the board were made from the same material.

Fascinated, Allie reached out to inspect one of the pieces more closely.

'Daddy'll smack you if you touch his chess-set.'

Allie looked behind her to find a pyjama-clad Jason staring at her disapprovingly.

'Do you think he would?' she asked, smiling at the little boy. He looked a lot cuter when he was clean, she decided . . . well, not so clean, she amended, taking a closer look at him. There was a small patch of red on his chin and a much larger one on the front of his pyjama tops. It looked like ketchup, or perhaps spaghetti sauce. Whatever it was, it didn't look as though Jason had been forced to forgo his dinner.

In response to her question, the child nodded solemnly. 'He spanked me.'

Allie's eyebrows shot up, then she frowned slightly. She was no expert on children, but she didn't think parents should have to resort to physical punishment to discipline their offspring. Surely there was a more civilised way of handling the situation?

She looked back at the chess-set and the boy came over to join her. 'That's the king,' he said, pointing with his finger, but keeping it a discreet quarter of an inch from the piece.

It was the strangest thing. Although her eyes were on the boy, she knew the moment Linc entered the room, even though his footfalls were silenced by the thick carpeting. Allie glanced away from the board and looked over to him. He was smiling as he walked over to them, his strides long and panther-like. A frisson of pleasure danced down her spine. What was it about him that made him so much more attractive than the other men Clare had introduced her to? Allie had accepted several invitations from the various men she'd met at Clare's barbecue, had enjoyed her outings with them, and yet . . . In the back of her mind, hadn't she wished that it had been Linc who had asked her out, had spent the evening with her, had kissed her goodnight?

Before Linc reached them, Jason commanded Allie's attention again by tugging at her arm. He'd succumbed to temptation and was holding one of the

chess-men. 'This looks like a horse, but it's called a
night. Isn't that stupid?' He giggled. 'Ta-ta-lum-ta-ta-
lumpt.' He galloped the little figurine across the palm
of his hand and up his arm.

When he looked up and saw his father, his game
ceased abruptly. His fingers curled around the chess-
man in an attempt to conceal it within his palm as he
met Linc's stern gaze with a sullen face. There was a
tense silence that seemed to stretch for hours, then the
man said in a low, dangerous voice, 'Put that back
where you found it.'

The boy's mouth set in a mutinous line. 'I was just
showing it to the lady,' he said sulkily, setting the
knight back on to its square with a clatter.

Allie saw Linc flinch and slid her gaze to the board,
making a furtive inspection of the chess-piece. It
didn't appear to have been damaged, but she did
notice that one or two of the other pieces had fine
cracks bisecting them. They appeared to have been
broken and glued back together. So it wasn't just a
dictatorial whim that had made Linc place the chess-
set out of bounds to his son.

However, his tone was conversational as he asked
the boy, 'Aren't you supposed to be in your room?'

'I was bored. There's nothing to do in there.'

Linc threw Allie a wry glance. 'He makes it sound
like Siberia. The toy department at Eaton's during
Christmas would be a better description.'

'I don't have hardly *any* toys!' Jason protested in
outrage. 'I don't have a "Snake Mountain" like
Darryl does. *And* he has——'

'You have enough,' his father cut him off abruptly.
'It's time you were back in your room, son. In case
you forgot, you were supposed to stay in there
because you didn't keep near the house this afternoon

as you were told to.'

'Ah, Dad,' he whined. 'Can't I stay up? My favourite programme's coming on. I want to watch TV.'

'No TV tonight. It's almost bedtime anyway, so off you get.'

Jason glared up at his father stubbornly. Allie could almost see him digging his heels in for a confrontation. Hastily, she intervened, 'How would it be if I read Jason a story in his room? You wouldn't mind, would you, Linc?'

Before he could answer, his son pre-empted him, shouting, 'I don't want a story! I hate books! They're stupid. I want to watch TV!'

'That's it, Jason!' Linc roared. 'You'll apologise to Miss Smith for being rude, and then you're going straight to your room.'

'I won't!' the boy retorted. 'I won't 'pologise! I want to watch TV!' he wailed.

He was nearly hysterical, his breath coming in jerky, hiccuping sobs. Quickly scooping Jason off his feet, Linc started to carry him from the room. Over his shoulder, he said to Allie, 'I'll be back in a few minutes.' The child was struggling in his arms, twisting and flailing his limbs, but Linc managed to retain his hold as he bore him away.

CHAPTER FIVE

IT WAS over half an hour before Linc returned to the living-room. As he walked in, Allie rose from the sofa where she had been idly flipping through a magazine, asking, 'Is he all right?'

Linc nodded. 'He's dropped off to sleep now.' There was a brooding air about him, his face was slightly pale and he looked older somehow. Allie felt her heart go out to him. She'd done a lot of thinking about him while he'd been out of the room settling his son down. In the past few weeks, Clare had let drop quite a few titbits about Linc's life. On the surface, he seemed to lead a charmed existence, the sort that would incite envy in other men and conceit within himself. He owned a successful computer programming firm in Vancouver, had this beautiful waterfront home. From the windows of the living-room she'd glimpsed a cabin cruiser moored below the house, and a single-engine float-plane. Clare had told her that he used them to commute between the island and his business in downtown Vancouver.

And it wasn't just materially that Linc had been blessed, Allie thought, looking over to him now. He was probably the most attractive man she'd ever encountered: lean, sexy, charming when he wanted to be. As an eligible bachelor, he could have his pick of women.

'I really want to apologise to you for that scene,' he said, breaking into her thoughts. He ran his hand through the dark pelt of his hair.

'Please, don't worry about it,' Allie said quickly. 'I'm just glad everything is OK.' It was a stupid comment. Of course everything wasn't OK. In many ways Jason was an appealing child, but he obviously had some problems, too. It couldn't be easy for Linc to cope with him. His life wasn't the bed of roses a casual observer might think it was.

For a moment it looked as though Linc might continue with the topic of Jason, but then he shrugged, looking away from Allie briefly. When he looked back, he asked, 'Look, I know this has kind of delayed dinner, but would you care to have a drink before we go into the dining-room? I should have asked you before.'

The truth was that Allie was famished. Her stomach was getting quite cranky from neglect. If she fed it alcohol now, it would probably send it straight to her head in a fit of pique.

On the other hand, if ever a man looked as if he needed a drink, it was Linc. Moving to resume her seat on the sofa, she said, 'That would be very nice. I wouldn't mind a glass of white wine.'

He nodded and moved to the drinks cabinet in the corner. Its polished wood doors concealed a small bar-fridge, and he retrieved ice and a bottle of wine from its recesses. After pouring Allie's glass of wine and handing it to her, he fixed his own drink: a generous splash of Canadian Club on the rocks. Taking a tiny sip of her own drink, Allie watched Linc take a hefty swallow of his before seating himself at the other end of the couch.

They sat in silence: Linc moodily savouring his whiskey, Allie taking minute swallows of wine in hopes that it would keep her stomach from rumbling.

After several minutes had elapsed, Linc roused himself. The magazine Allie had been thumbing through was lying on the sofa cushion that separated them. He picked it up and looked at it, then looked at Allie.

'Was this all you could find to read? I'm sorry about that. You must have found it boring.'

The magazine was the *New Scientist*. Although she had never subscribed to the British publication, she did read it occasionally, enjoying its articles on the latest happenings in the world of science.

She looked over to Linc, a small frown pleating her forehead. It was far from boring. She was about to tell him so when he looked up from the cover of the magazine and over to her. 'Mrs Dorcus usually has some fashion magazines lying around. I guess she must have put them away.'

'Oh . . .' She'd almost forgotten! She wasn't supposed to be the kind of girl who read even mildly intellectual publications. She wouldn't enjoy them and certainly wouldn't understand what they were about. 'The magazine was fine. I read the cartoons and looked through the pictures,' Allie said quickly.

Mrs Dorcus served them a delicious chicken casserole in the dining-room, and as Allie sent it down to her grateful tummy she wondered why she had been so hasty to reinforce Linc's delusions about the level of her intelligence. On moving out of Clare's home, she had half decided to drop her act of the dumb blonde. It had worked in the sense that her social life had never been so active. On the other hand, her dates would have been considerably more enjoyable if she hadn't had to restrict her comments to the totally insipid. The inevitable result had been that her escorts had been careful to gear their conversation to what they considered her level of understanding to be, and most of them had ended up boring her. While Allie hadn't exactly planned to advertise the fact that she had her doctorate in computer mathematics, she had decided that there must be some middle ground between that and appearing mentally deficient.

Allie glanced briefly over to Linc. He hadn't said much to her since they had sat down to the meal. Maybe it was only that he was preoccupied with thoughts concerning his son, but it could be that he could think of no common ground between them on which to base a conversation.

But Allie knew that there was a lot they could talk about. She loved to play chess . . . there was the magazine article she had been reading earlier, and of course Linc's business. He was even in the same field as she was! They had a lot in common, if only Linc knew it.

Maybe it was time that she let him know it. As Allie cleared her plate, she pondered the best way to open a conversation with him. She could hardly blurt out, 'Gee, Linc, I'm really smart, so you can talk to me about anything you want and I'll be able to understand it.' She needed to be a little more subtle than that!

'Shall we have our coffee out on the veranda?' Linc asked, breaking into her reverie.

'Yes, that would be lovely,' Allie agreed readily. It would also give her a few more minutes to think up a brilliant conversational gambit.

Allie never had been very successful in social exchanges, though, and the extra time only meant that she was able to formulate and reject several opening statements without coming up with one she was happy with. They had been on the veranda sipping cups of hot coffee for several minutes when, in desperation, she finally decided to just open her mouth and see what came out.

'Linc——'

'I was——' He spoke at the same moment as Allie, and they both halted abruptly. A space of several seconds passed, before Linc said, 'Sorry I interrupted you. What were you about to say?'

'I . . . er . . .' Allie stammered awkwardly, feeling her face grow warm for no good reason. 'It wasn't important. Please, what were you about to say?'

He laughed softly and she read his thoughts. They were acting like a couple of adolescent teenagers on their first date—awkward, overly polite to one another. While it might not be too far off the mark as far as she was concerned, she bet it was a unique experience for Linc. He didn't strike her as the type of man who was normally ill at ease in the company of a woman.

Somehow, knowing that he shared her tension helped to dissipate it, and she was able to answer easily when he asked, 'I was just going to ask how you think you'll like living out here in Cedar? We haven't many amenities out here, and it's a fair drive into Nanaimo.'

'I think I'm going to like it,' Allie told him. 'I've never lived in the country before, but I'm not much of a city person either. The last place I lived was just a small town.' She hesitated. It was a perfect opportunity to tell him about herself. Henning *was* just a small town: so small that its only claim to fame was that the Institute was located there. Once he knew that was where she had lived, it would be only natural for him to ask her about the Institute. She could tell him that that was where she'd worked, talk about her job there.

Yet something held her back and she felt almost relieved when Linc moved on with the conversation, talking about Cedar and the people who were her new neighbours. She watched him as he spoke, her thoughts jumbled. Why hadn't she seized the opportunity to set him straight? She'd hated her reputation as an 'egghead', but being treated like the village idiot wasn't any better. Why hadn't she told him?

'They say he had a fatal attraction for women.'

His words startled Allie out of her inattention to what he was saying. 'Who?' Unconsciously she'd been studying him, noting the way his dark hair curled at the nape of his neck, the tiny scar that marred the clean line of his jaw. That phrase—fatal attraction for women—it suited him to a T. Now she knew why she hadn't told him about the Institute, why she'd hedged earlier when he'd made the remark about the science magazine boring her.

His was a fatal attraction, and she had succumbed to it. Somewhere along the line she'd fallen in love with him. She couldn't tell him about herself now; she couldn't risk it. It would be fatal if he rejected her.

'I was telling you about Brother XII—the guy who named this area Cedar-by-the-Sea. Weren't you listening?'

She moistened her lips. 'Yes, of course I was. You just lost me there for a minute, that's all. Now, who was Brother XII again?'

He gave Allie a long look of exasperation, then with patient resignation went back over the ground he'd already covered. It seemed that Brother XII was a conman-cum-religious leader in the late nineteen-twenties who came to Vancouver Island to set up a commune with his followers. Later, the commune was moved to one of the offshore islands. Setting aside his coffee-cup and motioning for Allie to follow him, Linc moved to the railing of the veranda so he could point it out to her.

'You can see the island from here . . . no, not there, that one over to the right.' Linc slipped his arm around her waist to position her so that she could better follow his directioning. It was a singularly unhelpful gesture of assistance. With that hard, muscular arm about her, Allie couldn't take in anything but Linc's nearness. The faint scent of his aftershave filled her nostrils, the beating of her own pulse filled her ears.

'Unfortunately for the members of his cult, he was more interested in their money than their salvation. He milked them out of thousands of dollars and, when he'd milked them dry, tried to turn them off his settlement. In the end, they turned on him and he was forced to flee. He dynamited most of the buildings in the commune before sailing away. He hasn't been heard from since, although it's reputed that he left his wealth in gold buried either here in Cedar or on his island. Nobody's ever found it, although a lot have looked.'

For several moments, they looked out across the water to the mysterious Brother XII's island. Linc's arm was still around her, and Allie could feel its warmth burning through the thin material of her dress. Slowly his other arm came up and he linked them about her waist, drawing her back against his chest. She could feel his breath stir her hair and steeled herself to remain rigid in his hold. With her newly realised love, she feared her response if she were to allow it. She would betray herself.

As Linc eased her around to face him, Allie spoke quickly. 'You didn't finish your story. You never told me about Brother XII's attraction for women. What did you mean?'

Linc's eyes held hers in a steady gaze. He knew she was stalling, trying to distract him from kissing her. Her whole body ached for the touch of his lips on hers, but he'd only kissed her as a joke that morning. She hadn't found it funny, though.

He was probably no more serious about it now than he had been then—and she still wouldn't be able to take it as a light-hearted gesture.

His mouth quirked into a waiting smile, but he indulged her. 'It seems that most of Brother XII's disciples were women. There's a story of one woman he met on a train while travelling across the country. She was a very respectable young matron, married to a New York banker. She fell under Brother XII's spell and deserted her husband to live with him on his island.'

He lowered his head and his breath brushed against her temples. 'How does love on a beautiful island sound to you, Allie?' he asked softly.

The husky timbre of his voice flicked over her raw nerve-ends. Her mouth was dry as she averted her gaze from his. She didn't want him to read the answer in her eyes, to discover that, as long as he was the man, love in the middle of a parched desert would be heaven.

He raised a finger to her chin, turning her face back to his. Allie kept her lashes lowered and felt the warm caress of his mouth as it gently touched her lips. Hopelessly, she knew that she was lost. Her hands crept up his chest and she rested her palms against his shoulders. She didn't, she couldn't push him away, though. Her lips softened in invitation, her mouth parted to receive his kiss.

There was no kiss. Instead his arms dropped from around her and he stepped back. Confused, Allie looked up into his face. He gave her a wry smile, then said, 'I guess I'd better answer that before whoever it is wakes up Jason. Mrs Dorcus must be watching television in her room and can't hear it.'

Hear what? Allie wondered. However, at that moment, she heard the peal of the doorbell coming from inside the house. Leaving her with a nod of apology, Linc left the veranda through the living-room door. Alone, Allie made a face to herself. She supposed she had been literally saved by the bell. The kiss had ended before it had really got started, so she'd been spared making a fool of herself by melting all over Linc like an ice-cream cone in the sun. Somehow, though, she couldn't find it in her heart to feel very grateful to his visitor for interrupting them.

Allie walked to the house, pausing at the door. Although he and his guest were still in the hall, she could hear them talking. 'Well, I'm not exactly busy, but I have a guest,' Linc said. 'Allie Smith came over for dinner.'

'Allie?' came the response in sharp, feminine tones. 'Isn't that Clare's friend, who talked you into renting your cabin to her?'

'Yes, she's renting the cabin.'

'Oh, Linc!' the voice chided, and this time Allie recognised it as belonging to Elaine. 'I thought you went to all that trouble fixing the place up just so she wouldn't have an excuse to be over here bothering you all the time?'

'I never said that exactly,' Linc denied. Allie, nurturing a growing feeling of humiliation, wondered what *exactly* he had said. After all, he must have said something along those lines for Elaine to make a statement like that. Linc continued, 'I invited her to dinner. She just moved in today and hasn't had a chance to get organised yet.'

The couple entered the living-room. Although Allie was standing in full view of the doorway leading to the veranda, Elaine's attention was on Linc and she didn't notice her. 'You shouldn't let people take advantage of you. Now she'll probably be over here all the time expecting you to wait on her,' the other woman predicted. 'You should have let her fend for herself. You're too soft-hearted for your own good. You really need someone to look out for you!'

And I guess we all know who Elaine thinks that should be! Allie thought angrily, stung by the woman's remarks. At that moment, Elaine caught sight of her. The older woman's face flushed an unbecoming shade of fuchsia before she greeted Allie heartily, 'Why, hello, Allie! Linc and I were just discussing a mutual acquaintance of ours.' There was an awkward little silence as that ludicrous falsehood settled and Elaine regained her composure, her colour returning to normal. Finally she treated Allie to a charming smile, asking kindly, 'How are you tonight? I hear that this was moving day.'

Somewhat disconcerted by the other woman's insincere overtures, Allie murmured a response to her greeting, then shot a look at Linc. Unlike Elaine, he was still looking decidedly discomfited. Perhaps it was because he knew she couldn't possibly have swallowed Elaine's feeble explanation of her unflattering remarks, or maybe it was just the situation in general. After all, his girlfriend couldn't be too pleased with him after discovering that he had invited another woman to have dinner with him.

And it wasn't only dinner on the menu, either, Allie thought with a flush of bitterness. Who knew what Elaine would have stumbled in on if she'd delayed her arrival for another half hour? Allie certainly hadn't been thinking about her in the moments Linc had held her in his arms while they were out on the veranda, and apparently neither had he.

Linc was a real louse, now that she thought about it. He hadn't struck her as the philandering type, but then, as Clare was always telling her, Allie didn't know an awful lot about men. She *did* know that it was common knowledge that Linc was involved with Elaine, though. Wasn't one woman enough for him?

'It was such a lovely evening, I thought I'd drive out and beg a cup of coffee from you,' Elaine went on, ignoring the heavy atmosphere in the room as she slipped her arm confidently through Linc's. 'Have you had yours yet?'

'As a matter of fact, we have, although I'm sure we could go for another cup.' He deftly disengaged his arm from Elaine's possessive hold. 'I'll go fix a fresh pot and bring in some cups.' He looked relieved to have found an excuse to escape.

However, before he could leave the room, Elaine forestalled him. 'Oh, has Mrs Dorcus finished for the day?'

'Yes, she has. I told her I wouldn't be needing her any more tonight.'

'Really, Linc, you spoil that woman,' Elaine admonished, ignoring the fact that it was nearly nine-thirty at night and the housekeeper's day probably started at seven in the morning. She walked over to Linc, recapturing his arm in hers, this time giving it a little squeeze. 'I'll get the coffee.' She turned to look at Allie. 'I have a special way of making it. It comes out quite extraordinarily good, if I do say so myself.'

Allie had no intention of spending what was left of the evening watching Linc's girlfriend drool all over him—no matter how fantastic her coffee was! 'Perhaps I can sample it another time,' she said quickly, snatching her own opportunity to escape. 'I still have tons of stuff to unpack, and I really should be getting on with it.'

'Oh, of course, I understand,' the other woman replied graciously, not that Allie had expected any coaxing from Elaine to get her to stay.

She didn't expect to encounter any protests from Linc either, although in this she was wrong. 'You don't need to rush off. I'll come over in the morning to help you with your unpacking.'

It was hard to say who looked more put out by Linc's offer, Allie or Elaine. However, Elaine recovered first. 'Why, that's a lovely idea. I'll help, too. I haven't got much planned for tomorrow. You know, when I helped Linc with the design of the kitchen, I had in mind where things should go to make it as convenient as possible. If I help you unpack, I can make sure that things are put in the right places.'

'I couldn't put you to all that bother,' Allie protested, appalled by this turn of events. She'd rather live out of boxes for the next three months than have Elaine dictating where she should stow her dishes.

'It wouldn't be any bother. In fact, it'll probably be kind of fun.'

Fun wasn't exactly what Allie would expect out of a morning spent in Elaine's company. How was she going to put her off? She cut Linc a pleading glance, but there was no help in that quarter. In fact, he seemed quite unaware of her dilemma. He probably thought she wanted Elaine's help! Men were so dense at times.

In one last desperate attempt to get herself out of the fix she found herself in, Allie said, 'As a matter of fact, I'll probably have it finished by morning. I'm feeling in the mood to tackle it tonight.' She started quickly across the room to retrieve her bag from the end-table by the couch. Clutching it in her hands, she turned to face the couple. 'You two just stay here and enjoy your coffee. You both must have had full days, and you need a chance to relax.'

'What with moving, your day hasn't been exactly slack. You should be relaxing as well,' Linc protested. 'Besides, it's too late to start unpacking now.'

Allie could cheerfully have strangled him. When he walked over to her and moved to take the bag from her hands, she tightened her grip, as though confronted by a mugger. 'I'm leaving now, Linc,' Allie said abruptly. She saw a flicker of annoyance cross Linc's face, but there was little she could do about it. Tact hadn't been getting her anywhere. 'Don't worry about my unpacking. I'll handle it. Thank you for dinner, and it was nice seeing you again, Elaine.' She managed a travesty of a smile in the direction of the other woman.

This time Linc didn't try to delay her, although she wasn't exactly pleased by his suggestion that he walk her home. However, when she protested, he gestured towards the windows. 'It's almost dark. You'll need a flashlight on the path, so I'll come with you. Elaine can get the coffee started while I'm gone.'

Linc would never make a success of it in the diplomatic corps, Allie thought, as she accompanied him from the house. Neither she nor Elaine were happy with this latest move of his.

They walked in silence towards the base of the bluff, but before starting up the path through the woods Linc halted. Since he was in charge of the flashlight, and the path was a pitch-black tunnel through the trees, Allie had little choice but to stop as well.

'Look, Allie, why don't you have an early night? I think you're tired,' he said, putting his own explanation on her earlier shortness. 'Elaine and I don't mind helping you unpack tomorrow.' She saw the flash of his teeth in the twilight as he smiled at her.

He was like a dog with a meaty bone! Allie thought in annoyance. Why couldn't he just drop it? 'I can fend for myself,' Allie snapped, throwing Elaine's words at him. 'I don't want to take advantage of your soft heart.'

He stood quietly while she glared up at him. Finally she heard him sigh. 'I'm sorry you heard Elaine's unfortunate remarks. I wish you wouldn't take them seriously. I'm afraid Elaine has always been something of a mother hen where I'm concerned. Years ago she was my secretary, and I guess she's never got out of the habit of guarding my time.'

'How nice for you,' she sneered. And Linc thought *she* was dumb. Any fool could see that Elaine's feelings for him were neither maternal, nor leftover loyalty from the time he was her boss. She didn't want Linc doing things for Allie for the same reason any woman didn't want her man doing things for another woman.

'Look, Allie, can't you climb down off your high horse and meet Elaine half-way? I know she's embarrassed and regrets that you heard what she said.

'I was hoping you and she would hit if off. Elaine has a hard time making friends, partly because she does have a tendency to put her foot in her mouth every once in a while. She really didn't mean to hurt your feelings. By offering to help you tomorrow, she's trying to make amends.'

Amends, my foot! Allie thought. She just wants to keep her eye on you!

'Couldn't you try to be friends with her?' Linc coaxed.

'No, I couldn't,' she blurted out, sick to death of the conversation. Her voice crackling with ice, she continued, 'Look, Linc, you yourself told me not to make a nuisance of myself. I don't intend to, and I'd appreciate it if you would stop making a nuisance of *yourself*.'

'Allie!'

'I'd like to go back to the cabin now,' she stated hardily.

For a moment, Linc didn't reply, although his growing anger was a tangible element in the air about them. Suddenly he pushed the flashlight into her hand. 'Then you can damn well go. Sorry I delayed you.' Turning on his heel, he stalked off into the darkness.

CHAPTER SIX

IN THE week that followed, Allie settled into her new home. The day after her dinner with Linc, which was a Sunday, she finished her unpacking. It seemed like a lonely and tedious job as she did it alone. However, it would have been worse having Elaine there to make sure she was putting everything in the 'right' places!

The rest of the week was dedicated to setting up her office. Although she wasn't currently employed anywhere, she knew she would go mad if she didn't find some project to work on over the summer. Already the thrill of partaking in an active social life was beginning to pale, and she was growing restive. Her whole life had been devoted to work, first at school and later in her job. She couldn't just quit 'cold turkey'.

Consequently, she started looking for some kind of computer program she could develop on a freelance basis. A couple of possibilities presented themselves. There was a need in the forest industry for a program that would 'understand', record and compile vocal signals sent in from hand-held walkie-talkies. It would be used by the scalers who went through the forest counting and measuring the trees to estimate the lumber in them.

The second sounded more challenging to Allie. Salmon-farming was a growing industry in British Columbia. Echo-sounders, working much like a sonar, could be used to count the number of fish in a tank, but a computer was needed to analyse the data. Developing the program wasn't as simple as it might first appear. The sounder recorded not only the fish, but also any air bubbles present in the tank. The program had to be able to distinguish between fish and bubbles. Further difficulties arose when the fish were massed together, making individual reportings indistinguishable, or, if some of them moved to a different location while the readings were being taken, they would then be counted twice or missed altogether.

In the end, Allie decided to tackle the salmon-counting problem. It looked as if it could be an all-absorbing one. Although she hated to admit it even to herself, she knew she needed something that would take up all her time and occupy all her thoughts. Her infatuation with Kevin had left a few scars, but they had healed swiftly upon coming to Vancouver Island. She seldom even thought of him now—and, when she did, she wondered what she'd ever seen in him!

Unfortunately, she didn't think she was going to get over Linc quite so easily. Although she refused to accept that her feelings for him were anything more than another infatuation, she knew there was a quality and depth to them that she hadn't felt when she had thought she was in love with Kevin. Linc would be harder to forget.

It didn't help matters to know that he was so close. She'd discovered that by standing in a certain spot in the upstairs loft and craning her neck to peer through the high window in the peak of the roof she had a view of his veranda and the moorage in front of his house. Even if she hadn't heard his float-plane leaving every morning and returning each afternoon, she could see whether he was home.

That knowledge led her into a rather embarrassing moment of weakness. She still had Linc's flashlight and, although she'd vowed she wasn't going to seek him out, on Thursday evening she started down the path connecting their houses with the excuse of returning it. His plane had returned earlier, so she knew he had returned from his work day in Vancouver.

As she waited for him to answer the doorbell, Allie mentally reviewed what she planned to say to him. She supposed she owed him an apology for the argument they'd had on Saturday night. Since it had centred on Elaine, she wasn't feeling particularly repentant or apologetic, but she had to get it over with if she and Linc were ever going to reach any kind of understanding. She'd been terribly rude and ungracious about his offer to help.

The door was answered by Mrs Dorcus. Linc's housekeeper was a lean, spare woman in her fifties with a hatchet face and mouse-brown hair liberally sprinkled with grey, twisted into a severe bun. Linc had told Allie that his son had her wrapped around his little finger, but it was rather hard to believe that.

'Miss Smith, how do you do?' she greeted Allie politely, stepping back from the doorway to allow Allie to enter the hall.

'I just stopped in to drop Linc's flashlight off,' Allie said awkwardly. The house was very quiet and, looking past the housekeeper's shoulder, Allie could see that the living-room appeared to be deserted. Was Linc out . . . with Elaine? She had to know. 'I thought I might have a word with Linc, if he's in,' she said, handing over the flashlight.

Mrs Dorcus said stiffly, 'He's in the study working this evening. I'll tell him you're here.'

'It's not that important,' Allie said quickly, but the older woman had already moved off down the hall. She had a sinking feeling in the pit of her stomach. She shouldn't be here. Linc wasn't going to like having to take time out from his work just to talk to her. It was too late now, though. Allie saw the housekeeper knock on a door at the far end of the hall, and faintly heard a curt voice bid her enter.

Mrs Dorcus returned a few minutes later. Was it Allie's imagination, or had her severe features grown even colder. 'I'm afraid Mr Summerville is tied up right now. He suggested you wait with me for a few minutes, then he will be out to see you. May I get you something . . . tea, coffee?'

'Oh, please, don't bother. I'll be going. As I said, it wasn't all that important.' Allie practically dived out of the front door. Linc wouldn't be expecting her to wait. Why had she come here? Hadn't he made it clear to her a number of times that he was a busy man, that he didn't want her bothering him? She cursed her stupidity all the way back to the cabin. She was an exceptionally intelligent woman—why didn't she ever act like one when it came to Linc?

For a long time she sat brooding on the rose-coloured chesterfield that Elaine had picked out and that Allie had decided she hated. The shadows lengthened, the room eventually falling into darkness. It was nearly midnight before she finally roused herself. Sitting around feeling sorry for herself wasn't getting anywhere. So, she loved Linc and he didn't love her . . . didn't even seem to like her very much. She still had her work.

Knowing she wouldn't sleep, Allie went up to the loft to see Harold. Greg had some contacts with the fishing industry and had got some data for her to use

in designing her fish-count program. Instead of
running after Linc, she should have stayed at home
and started feeding it into her computer. It was still
waiting for her. She would start on it tonight.

By afternoon the next day, Allie had a screaming
headache. The characters on the computer screen,
which usually held such fascination for her, kept
blurring before her eyes, sliding in and out of focus.
Typically, she'd forgotten to buy any aspirin, so she
didn't have anything for the pain. Finally, she gave up
trying to work and went downstairs to lie down for a
while. She'd had two, maybe three hours' sleep the
night before. A rest would probably do wonders for
her head.

But she couldn't rest. The heat in the small
bedroom was stifling, intensifying the throbbing in
her temples. She sat up on the bed and glared at the
window. Whoever had redecorated the cabin had
painted it shut. She'd tried several times to get it
open, but to no avail. She'd get it open somehow, she
vowed, swinging her legs over the side of the bed.

She didn't own any carpentry tools, not even a
screwdriver. However, she found a sharp knife in the
cutlery drawer and got a rock from outside to use as a
hammer. Leaving the back door open in the hope that
some of the heat from the bedroom would find its way
out, she went back to fix the window.

Using the knife as a chisel, she gently tapped it with
the rock to cut through the paint seal between the
window and the jamb. When the lower edge was free,
she set the tools aside and tried pushing the window
up.

Damn, it still wouldn't open. Growing impatient,
Allie wiped the sweat from her forehead with the back

of her hand, then positioned the knife along the side edge. Using her right hand, she gave the bottom of the knife-handle a hefty wallop with the rock. The rounded stone slid off the end of the knife and crashed into the window-pane, shattering it.

'Oh, hell!' Allie swore, automatically jerking the hand holding the rock back into the room. There was a great hole in the window, edged with wicked-looking shards of glass. Allie glanced at the rock and found herself staring at blood pouring from a jagged six-inch cut that snaked down the side of her hand and across her wrist. 'Oh, h-hell-ll,' she repeated, letting the rock fall.

The pain hit suddenly and she gasped, biting her lip between her teeth to keep from crying out. She managed to stagger over to the bed and sit down, cradling her injured arm against her side. Taking a deep breath, she gingerly turned her arm so that she could take another look at the cut. She took only a quick peep, then dropped the knife she'd been holding in her left hand on to the floor and clamped that hand over the wound. Closing her eyes for a moment, she fought off a feeling of faintness.

Trying to keep calm, Allie took stock of the situation. Along the side of her hand, the cut was little more than a scratch. Where it curved across her inner wrist, though, it was much deeper, and the blood poured from the wound whenever she took the pressure off it. It was obvious she needed some stitches, but how was she going to arrange it?

Her phone hadn't been connected yet, so she couldn't call anyone to help her. Even if she managed to make it to the car without further mishap, she couldn't possibly drive with her hand in this condition. All in all, it looked as if she might just sit here and bleed to death, because she had an awful feeling that she had nicked a vein.

That, however, was defeatist thinking. Things weren't all that bad. She hardly even noticed her headache any more. And, if there was no one to call on for help, she would just have to help herself.

Very slowly, Allie stood up. The room swooped dizzily for a moment, then settled. Keeping her left hand clamped tightly around her wrist, she moved carefully over to the dresser. She had to release her arm in order to pull open her lingerie drawer. With her left hand, she tossed out the frothy bits of nylon panties and bras until she found what she was looking for. Holding on to the tights, she gingerly made her way back to the bed.

Seated again, she straightened her injured arm, blinking back the tears of pain the action forced from her. Fumbling with the stocking, she awkwardly started to wrap it around her arm to make a tourniquet. Her fingers wouldn't do what she told them to, though, and the ends of material kept slipping away from them as she tried to tie them together. In the end, they eluded her altogether and the tights slipped to the floor.

Realising she was getting slightly panicky, she forced herself to relax for a moment and breathe deeply and evenly, using her uninjured hand to keep pressure on the wound. She was starting to feel decidedly light-headed, and she couldn't afford to pass out.

'Whatya doin'?'

The first time Jason had walked in unannounced and asked her that question, she'd thought him a rude, unmannerly little brat. However, this time she felt like kissing him when she turned her head and saw him standing in the doorway behind her.

'Jason, is your dad home?'

He shrugged, taking a step into the room. Quickly, Allie forestalled him. 'Don't come in.' Turning her shoulder away from him, she blocked his view of her arm. It wasn't a sight that a young child should be exposed to. 'Jason, would you run home really fast and get your daddy or Mrs Dorcus, and ask them to come back here?'

'How come?'

Allie moistened her lips. She'd forgotten that Jason had a maddening trait of questioning every request. 'I just want to talk with one of them. Couldn't you just do as I ask?'

'But how come?'

'Just get them, Jason. Please,' Allie pleaded, almost ready to burst into tears. A cold chill was creeping over her, and she didn't think it had anything to do with the fresh air coming in through the broken window. Probably her blood-pressure was dropping from loss of blood. She looked down at her arm. Crimson was seeping through the fingers of her left hand.

When she looked up again, Jason was standing right in front of her. He was looking down at her cradled wrist, his face puzzled. 'You hurt yourself.' He sounded intrigued, but thankfully not traumatised. 'Daddy put a bandage on my knee when I cut it. You want him to put one on your arm?'

Allie nodded, tears of relief filming her grey eyes. She had been beginning to think he would keep her arguing all afternoon.

As Jason turned to leave, they heard his name being called from outside. 'There's Dad now,' the child announced, and dashed out of the room.

Within a few moments, Allie heard them enter the cabin through the kitchen. 'Come *on*, Dad!' Jason chided. 'She wants you——'

'Didn't I tell you not to keep coming over here and bothering Miss Smith?' his father interrupted him sternly.

'But, Dad, she needs a bandage!' Jason protested, dragging his father into the bedroom by his hand.

Allie looked over at him, offering him a fragile smile. Although she subconsciously must have noticed it before, it hit her full force just how *reliable* Linc looked. The panicky feeling that had been growing within her ever since she'd seen the blood died instantly with his arrival. With his firm jawline and direct gaze, he was a man she could depend on.

'I'm sorry about Jason coming over,' Linc offered, holding his ground at the doorway. 'He slipped away from me.' He smiled wryly.

'I was glad to see him. I do need a bandage,' she understated. She shifted her position on the bed so that he could see her arm.

For several seconds, Linc stared at her in stunned silence, the smile fading from his face. Then he was moving, his long legs carrying him in swift strides around the bed to stand in front of her. 'Good heavens, what happened?'

Allie shrugged. The story of the rock, the knife and the window-pane seemed so idiotic now that she thought about it. It wasn't hard to understand why he assumed she was a 'dumb blonde'. She was in a lot of ways.

His navy eyes had moved down from her arm to the floor by the bed. He reached down slowly and picked up the knife from where it had fallen at her feet. However, Allie was more intent on the dark stain of blood that marred the grey carpeting.

'I'm sorry about the carpet. I know it was new.'

Linc's face had lost its colour, and his eyes held a disturbing look as they met hers.

Damn, he wasn't going to pass out on her, was he? Allie thought in alarm. A lot of people, great hulking football players even, couldn't take the sight of blood. 'I guess I should have done this in the bathroom where I wouldn't have made such a mess,' Allie joked, trying to lighten the atmosphere.

'Yes,' he agreed grimly. His firm jaw had hardened to granite and a tiny pulse throbbed at his temple. But at least he didn't look as if he was going to faint. 'I'd always thought the bath was the traditional place.'

She didn't have a chance to figure out what he meant by that remark, because he placed his arm around her shoulders to get her to her feet. The movement disturbed her injury, and all her thought-processes became directed towards controlling the sudden upsurge of pain.

'Let's get you in the bathroom now, and I'll try to fix you up enough to drive you into the hospital.' He looked over to his son. 'You go home and stay with Mrs Dorcus. Tell her I don't know when I'll be back.'

'It was good of you to wait, but I guess they're going to make me stay in here tonight.'

Using her left hand, Allie distractedly fingered the nap of the blanket covering her, then ceased the movement as she felt a twinge of discomfort. Her right hand was swathed in bandages, but this hand hadn't totally escaped. Tape covered it, holding the needle from the transfusion bottle hanging beside the hospital bed in place.

When Linc made no reply, Allie went on, 'I hate

these places. I wish I could go home.' She knew she was chattering inanely, but she felt so awkward in Linc's company that she couldn't seem to help herself. What were you supposed to say to someone who had probably saved your life? Especially when you'd made an ass out of yourself afterwards.

Linc had brought her into the emergency-room at the hospital several hours earlier. Before a medical person would even look at her, there were a million forms to fill out. The whole procedure had been complicated because she'd only recently moved to British Columbia and she was covered under another province's health insurance plan. Linc had managed to cut through the red-tape finally—which was a good thing, since she hadn't been much use. By that time, she'd been feeling pretty dreadful, what with the pain in her hand and the blood she'd lost.

Maybe that was why later she'd raised such a fuss when the doctor had tried to send Linc out of the room while he examined Allie's arm before stitching it up. She'd clung to Linc's hand with her uninjured one and refused to let him leave. In the end, he'd been forced to stay and watch the whole gruesome procedure.

Later on, though, she'd let him go while the nurses cleaned her up and put her in one of those ghastly hospital nightgowns. They'd given her a shot of something and afterwards she'd fallen asleep. She hadn't really expected Linc to still be there when she woke up. However, he was sitting in a chair by her bed when she opened her eyes.

'Hospitals aren't that bad. Maybe you ought to plan to stay a few days,' Linc suggested.

Allie grimaced. 'I don't think that's necessary. I'll be fine by tomorrow. They're only keeping me in for this.' She gestured to the transfusion apparatus.

Linc hesitated before speaking and she gave him a curious look. At last, he said, 'Are you sure about that . . . about being fine, I mean?'

'Of course.' She had to admit it gave her a little thrill to think that he was so concerned about her. It was tempting to lie here and play the frail Camille, even if that wasn't really her style. Unfortunately, though, concern made Linc look frightfully grim. 'I'll be right as rain tomorrow,' she assured him brightly.

He gave her a searching look filled with doubt. However, he veered on to a new topic when he spoke. 'You should have waited to see me last night. I was in the middle of an important phone call when Mrs Dorcus came in to tell me you were there. I would have seen you afterwards if you had waited.'

'It wasn't that important, and I didn't want to bother you.'

His firm mouth pursed in exasperation. 'I wish I'd never said that to you! I'll admit that I do have a lot to do, but nothing I do is *that* important.' His eyes moved to her bandaged hand and arm, staring at it so intently that Allie felt he was almost blaming himself for the accident. 'I want you to promise me that next time you need someone to talk to, you'll come to me. I'll make time to see you. I don't mind.'

Allie was taken aback by his vehemence. 'OK,' she said meekly. Perhaps he *was* blaming himself for what had happened, although there was no need. Even if they had been on better terms, she might not have asked him to fix the window. She'd acted on impulse, spurred on by the heat in the bedroom. It really wasn't Linc's fault.

Before she could explain, though, he went on, 'I want you to think seriously about staying on here in the hospital for a couple of weeks. They can do a lot to help you. I know you've had a rough time of it lately, what with being out of work and all. I'm afraid that Clare let slip that you'd been involved with some man before you came here and the relationship had gone sour. But you can't let it beat you!' Linc declared passionately, leaning forward in his chair. Mindful of the transfusion needle, he gingerly grasped the fingers of her left hand and stroked them gently. 'People still care about you. Clare and Greg . . . myself—we care. Your life has value.'

Allie's mouth had been dropping slowly throughout his speech. She managed to close it and swallowed deeply. 'What are you talking about?' She saw he was looking at her bandaged hand again. 'You don't think . . . you're not thinking . . . it was a dumb thing to do, but I'm not suicidal! I didn't put that rock through the window on purpose!'

'What rock? What window? All I saw was a knife!'

'And you think I tried to slash my wrists with it?' she sputtered, outraged. Realising he still had her fingers in his grasp, she jerked them free, glaring at him.

'Didn't you?'

'Don't be daft!' Allie enjoined. 'I was trying to get the window open. It was painted shut and I was using the knife to cut through the seal, only I needed something to use for a hammer so I found a rock. When it slipped, it took my hand with it through the pane. You must have seen the broken window!'

Linc slowly shook his head. He looked dazed, but that forbidding bleakness had left his expression. 'When I saw all that blood, and the knife lying at your feet . . . nothing else in the room registered.'

His eyes searched her face and Allie found her anger

slipping away. She couldn't hang on to it. He had jumped—no, positively bounded—to the wrong conclusion, but he had obviously been very upset by that conclusion. He'd told her he cared about her. She didn't think it had just been part of his pep-talk. He'd sounded as if he really meant it. Her smile warmed her grey eyes.

Feeling happier with him, she was caught off guard by his sudden spurt of wrath. Standing abruptly, he strode to the door, then turned back and stalked over to look down at her. 'Why didn't you ask me to fix the window for you?'

'I didn't want to bother you.'

Linc snorted, turning his back on her. 'You bother me whether you want to or not!'

That was a hateful thing to say, and Allie's lower lip quivered as she battled with hurt tears. Linc turned his head to slash her a look, and saw her expression. 'Oh, hell!' he swore fiercely. Suddenly, he braced his hands on either side of her head and bent over her, his mouth covering hers.

It was a firm, demanding, unexpected kiss. Unprepared for it, Allie felt unchecked response explode within her. Her lips, soft and warm, moved beneath his, savouring the taste of him. She could hear his breath quicken in tune with her own, a low groan in his throat. His mouth slid from hers, along her cheek to her eyes in soft, caressing kisses. 'You bother me, Allie. Oh, how you bother me,' he whispered. 'You fill my thoughts and drive me mad with wanting you.'

Carefully, he lowered himself to his elbows and cradled her head between his forearms. His mouth moved back to hers, drinking long and deep at that sweet fountain. At last, he lifted his head to look deep into her passion-drenched eyes. Wanting him as much as he wanted her, Allie made a movement to coax him back.

'This isn't the time or the place, darling. The nurse is going to come in here any minute and kick me out.' He smiled down at her as he stood upright. Gently stroking the smooth flesh of her injured arm above the bandages, he said, 'You're not going to be much good at looking after yourself until that's healed. I'll pick you up in the morning and take you home with me for a few days.'

Suddenly everything was moving too fast for Allie. Was this what she really wanted? She loved Linc, of that she was certain . . . and yet . . . She was suddenly afraid of taking the next step. This was the point where things had gone wrong with Kevin. If she slept with Linc, would he find her inadequate, unsatisfying?

'Maybe I should call Clare. It might be better if . . .'

She could see his withdrawal in his expression. 'I already called Clare to tell her about your accident. You can't stay at her place. She's got a houseful of relatives from Ontario. I gather that they're having to camp out in the living-room as it is. You'll have to stay with me . . . unless maybe Elaine could look after you?' He caught her grimace and treated her to a harsh look. 'I'd forgotten. You don't like Elaine much.'

Allie flinched at that barb. No, she didn't like his girlfriend! That was, if Elaine was his girlfriend, Allie thought, suddenly confused. He hadn't treated the other woman in a very lover-like manner the other evening, even though he had defended her. Besides, would Linc have kissed her like that, invited her to convalesce at his home, if he was involved with someone else? He wasn't that kind of man, was he?

She looked up at him. Suddenly she felt inordinately weary. The local anaesthetic the doctor had administered so that he could stitch up her hand was wearing off, and the cut throbbed painfully. She didn't know what she should think, what she should say to Linc.

He finally broke the uncomfortable silence. 'It wasn't an invitation to share my bed, Allie. Only my house, until your hand is healed. If you don't want to accept, then don't.' He swung around and started towards the door.

'Linc!' Allie called after him. At the sound of his name he turned back, one eyebrow cocked in enquiry as he regarded her. She moistened her lips. 'If the offer is still open, I'd like to stay with you.'

'It is,' he said flatly, giving no indication of his feelings on the matter.

'Then . . . er . . . thank you.'

'I'll pick you up in the morning.' With that, he turned and left the room. Allie lay on her pillow and stared up at the ceiling, too tired to sort out her tangled thoughts and emotions.

CHAPTER SEVEN

LINC slid the black Ford into the parking space and turned off the ignition. Slewing around in his seat, he gave Allie a frowning stare. 'You're sure the doctor said it would be OK for you to go home this morning?'

Self-consciously, Allie averted her face as she nodded her head, wishing she could wear a paper bag over it so he couldn't look at her. She knew what he was getting at. She didn't look well, what with every toss and turn of her restless night reflected in her violet-shadowed eyes and washed-out complexion. Maybe if she'd had more cosmetics she could have disguised the worst of the damages, but the lone tube of lipstick she'd found in her handbag hadn't been much help. When Linc had brought her into the hospital the previous afternoon, there hadn't been time to think of things like blusher and foundation. As it was, Linc had had to bring her in a clean shirt and slacks to wear home that morning.

Making no move to leave the car, he stayed looking at her with a doubtful expression on his well-formed features. 'I'm really fine,' Allie assured him. He didn't seem satisfied, so she continued, 'I didn't sleep very well. You know, a strange bed and nurses barging in and out all night.' She shrugged, hoping that the hospital staff who had looked after her so well would forgive her. It had been thoughts of Linc that had barged in, kept her from sleeping in what was actually a very comfortable bed.

'You should have asked one of them to give you something for the pain in your arm if it was bothering you.'

Damn, he must have noticed the pink tinge of her eyelids. She had shed a few tears during the long night, but they hadn't been from pain—at least, not from the physical pain of her cut wrist. They had been tears of confusion, of uncertainty, of an unfulfilled, aching need for him.

She looked up to meet his dark blue eyes resting on her, reading the gentle concern in them. Seeing that look, she knew she had come to the right decision after that long night of irresolution. Linc wasn't like Kevin. He was a kind, caring man. He'd never said he loved her, but perhaps that didn't matter. Words of love had come easily from Kevin—and had meant nothing. Linc had told her that he cared, that he wanted her. Coming from a man with his strength and integrity, that was worth far more than all that 'I love yous' in the world from a man like Kevin.

'You said the doctor gave you a prescription for pain-killers? You can wait in the car while I get it made up for you. Close your eyes for a few minutes and have a rest.'

'I told you, I'm fine. I'll handle it,' Allie said, unconsciously taking a firmer grip on her handbag where the prescription slips resided. She'd come to a decision, but still didn't know how she was going to let Linc know about it. However, letting him find out by seeing that, in addition to the prescription for pain-killing pills, the doctor had also given her one for birth-control pills didn't seem to be quite the way.

Linc's frown deepened and she knew he was about to argue. Quickly, Allie inserted, 'I've a couple of things to pick up at the chemist's. I need to go in myself.' Hoping to forestall him, she turned hastily to open the car door. Unfortunately, she'd forgotten about the sling on her right arm. Awkwardly, she twisted around to reach the handle with her left hand. The door was locked. When she stretched around to pull up the door-lock, though, she jarred her injured arm, and gasped. Biting her lip, she faced forward again, cradling her sore arm in her lap.

'Serves you right for being so damned independent,' Linc snarled heartlessly, reaching behind her to unlock the door. Instead of pulling his arm back, he let it drop across her shoulders. Despite the tone of his voice, his fingers were gentle as he stroked her upper arm. His touch sent a warm flood of sensation through Allie that blotted out the pain of her injury.

She turned her head and found his face was only inches from her own, his breath softly mingling with hers. His navy eyes darkened to midnight as they focused on her mouth, studying the motion of her tongue as she ran it over her suddenly dry lips. His head came closer, but to her disappointment his lips simply brushed the smooth curve of her cheek before he pulled back.

'You're sure you don't want me to run your errands while you rest?'

Allie blinked at him, dragging herself back to the prosaic. Finally, she shook her head. 'I'll do it myself.'

'Well, at least let me help you get out of the car,' Linc advised, opening the driver's side door and sliding out from behind the steering wheel.

Allie half feared that Linc would insist on coming into the shop with her. He helped her from the vehicle with all the care of a man handling fine porcelain, as though she might shatter on the pavement when her foot touched it. However, to her relief, he left her at the entrance to the pharmacy, suggesting she meet him for coffee in the café two doors down when she'd finished her shopping.

They didn't linger in the café. Although Allie didn't want to admit it, the few minutes spent in the chemist's had taxed her small store of energy to the limit. She was feeling a little as though she *was* made of fragile porcelain by the time she left to meet Linc for coffee. The hot liquid revived her somewhat, but she was none the less happy to go when Linc suggested they head for home after only a few minutes.

As they drove along, Allie stared silently out of the window at the passing scenery, her spirits sinking. Linc hadn't said much to her over coffee, and he'd been totally silent since they'd got back into the car. Maybe he hadn't hustled her from the restaurant with such speed because he had realised how tired she was. Maybe *he* had grown tired of wasting his whole morning on her. Although it was a Saturday, that didn't mean he didn't have work waiting for him. He didn't strike her as the type of man to confine his business to Monday through Friday. Even if he didn't have work he should be spending his morning on, he had a son. She sensed he was a conscientious, loving father. The free time that he had at the weekends to spend with his child was probably rare and precious to him.

And she was going to be intruding.

They were approaching the bend in the road around which lay the driveway to the cabin. Impulsively, Allie turned to Linc, touching his arm with her free hand to gain his attention. He glanced at her, then moved his eyes back to the road to negotiate the curve.

'Why don't you just drop me off at the cabin? I don't really need to stay with you. I've still got one good hand and I can manage.'

She saw Linc's lips firm, his eyes riveted on the road ahead. Without replying to her, he accelerated slightly as they passed the entrance to the cabin's driveway. Allie turned and watched it recede from view, before turning back to give Linc a vexed look. 'I asked you to stop,' she stated, pride and affront that he had ignored her request making her voice cold. 'I appreciate your giving me a lift from the hospital, but I'd like to go to my own home now.'

Linc slowed the car, but only to turn into the drive of his home. Still without speaking, he drove slowly down it to the house, then braked. Switching off the ignition, he turned to look at her. 'I thought we went over all this yesterday afternoon. You agreed to stay here.'

'Well, I changed my mind.'

'Then unchange it,' Linc ordered harshly. He glared at her for a moment, then sighed deeply. 'You know that as long as you're wearing that sling your right hand is useless. You can't manage on your own.'

Her grey eyes stormy, Allie turned her head away and stared down at her sling. He had a point. That morning, she'd managed to dress by herself, but the nurse had had to help her with buttons and zip, then reposition the sling. She'd also had to help her wash and comb her hair. Eating breakfast had been a challenge, since Allie had never tried to butter her toast with one hand before.

She could survive, though.

She knew Linc was watching her, but she stubbornly refused to look over to him. 'I just think it would be better all round if I went to my own place,'

Allie said quietly, but very firmly.

The moment of silence that followed was heavy with tension. Finally, Linc burst out, 'I'll probably strangle you if you tell me you don't want to impose on me. As for any qualms you may be having, I promised you that you'll be safe in my house. What more can I do—shave my head and don a monk's robe for the duration of your visit? So I've kissed you a couple of times. It doesn't mean you're irresistible. I'm not going to seduce you if you stay overnight in my house. I'm not interested. Your maidenly virtue will be perfectly safe!'

'I . . . I . . .' Allie stopped talking abruptly as his words crashed into her consciousness. Swiftly, she lowered her head so that he couldn't see the sudden tears that had sprung to her eyes. Through the blur of moisture she stared at the parcel from the pharmacy. Damn. Damn, damn, damn! She'd learned calculus and physics with the ease that most people memorised their home phone number. But she'd never learned anything from her relationship with Kevin, it seemed. She'd taken his kisses and conjured a full-scale love-affair out of them. He hadn't been interested, either—but she was boss, so he'd played along with her.

For whatever reason Linc had kissed her yesterday, had said he wanted her, he hadn't intended making love with her. He'd told her that then, only she'd been too stupid to believe him.

'Come on into the house, Allie,' he suggested quietly, the heat gone from his voice. 'You've had a rough morning and I think you're tired. You can have a nap before lunch. Mrs Dorcus brought back your clothes when she went over to the cabin to get something for you to wear home this morning.'

He got out of the car and walked around to her side to open the door for her. Avoiding the helping hand he held out to her, Allie scrambled as best she could from the vehicle and preceded him to the house. He was treating her like a child, a cranky child in need of her bed. It was pointless to keep arguing with him while he maintained that attitude. He'd probably either try to bribe her with a sweetie or spank her if she did! Pride raised her head to an aloof angle, as maintaining a semblance of dignity was about the only course left open to her.

Whether she was a cranky child or not, Allie felt much better after a sleep. She obviously needed the rest, since she slept through lunch and most of the afternoon. When she awoke, she was able to view the situation with greater equanimity. Linc was being a good friend to her, and, other than Clare, she didn't have many friends. Not only had Linc offered her his home to convalesce in, but he'd even arranged for Jason to spend the weekend with his grandparents so that the little boy's boisterousness wouldn't disturb her rest when she wasn't feeling up to par.

Viewed from that perspective, it was immature and ridiculous in the extreme for her to feel angry and resentful because he didn't feel anything *more* than friendship for her. After her break with Kevin, she'd accepted that she wasn't the sort of woman that men fell in love with. Maybe her pretence of being less intelligent that she really was had temporarily cajoled her into thinking otherwise, but inside she hadn't changed. Maybe Linc had sensed it. Maybe that was why, when Linc had said he cared, he'd only meant it as a friend.

It wasn't a particularly cheering thought, but, as

Allie pushed the covers back and swung her feet over
the side of the bed, she knew it was one she was going
to have to learn to live with. And she was going to
have to start treating Linc as a friend, because at least
his friendship was better than nothing.

She'd start at dinner, Allie vowed. Taking up her
robe from the end of the bed, she eased it over the
bandages covering her right hand and arm, then
looped the tie belt together with her left hand to hold
it loosely closed. The bathroom was only next door,
and she wanted a shower before dressing for dinner.
Fortunately, one of the dresses Mrs Dorcus had
brought over was still in its dry-cleaner's bag, and she
could use the plastic from it to keep her injured arm
dry.

She managed the shower without too much trouble,
as long as she remembered not to try to use her right
hand, encased in the plastic, for anything. The warm
cascade of water felt so good, in fact, that she decided
to go ahead and wash her hair. One-handed, she
awkwardly rubbed the shampoo through her hair,
then moved beneath the spray to rinse it away. The
foaming lather streamed down her face and into her
eyes, causing her to yelp in pain. Blindly, she fumbled
through the shower curtain to get a towel—and forgot
that her right arm had been injured.

Groaning as pain shot through the whole right side
of her body, Allie pulled her arm against her midriff,
holding it protectively. The next moment, the
shower-curtain was whipped aside and the water was
turned off.

Tears streaming from her closed eyes, Allie heard
Linc's voice ask in alarm, 'Are you all right? I heard
you cry out.'

'I've got shampoo in my eyes,' Allie explained,

rubbing them with the back of her left hand. Her
hand was pushed away, and Linc started drying her
face with a towel. When he'd finished, he lifted her
out of the bath. As she felt the soft cushion of the rug
beneath her feet, Allie gingerly opened her eyes,
relieved to find that they no longer smarted from the
light.

She pulled the plastic covering from her right arm,
then looked up at Linc, ready to apologise for
alarming him. The words never made it. He was still
holding the towel, forgotten, in his hands, and he was
staring at her. His eyes lingered over her firm, full
breasts, then glided lower to her waist, lower . . .

A hot flush of embarrassment burned over her, then
cooled when he raised his eyes back to her face. There
was no masking the naked desire that flamed within
them. Stunned, Allie stared back at him, her breath
growing shallow and ragged. The passionate flame
that flickered and flared in his navy eyes arced
between them to light an answering one in the depths
of her silvery grey ones. All thoughts of the friendly,
sisterly attitude she had resolved to take towards him
flew from her head. She could never accept him as a
friend when every cell within her ached for him as her
lover. Nothing else mattered.

His gaze was drawn to the irregular rise and fall of
her chest. The towel falling from his hand, he reached
out as though in slow motion and lay his palm over
the smooth curve of her breast. Beneath his hand,
Allie's heart thundered in a wild tattoo as she swayed
towards him.

'Allie,' he said hoarsely, seeking her eyes again.
'You're beautiful.' His hand moved gently over the
satin flesh, his fingers seeking the hard button of her
nipple, his palm dropping to cup the weight of her

breast. A wordless murmur of joy escaped from Allie as the electricity of his touch sparked through her.

The sound broke the spell the sight of her nude body had woven over him. Linc tensed, his hand falling to his side.

'My promise, Allie,' he reminded her, his tone agonised. 'You should tell me to leave. This isn't supposed to happen.'

For a long, tension-filled minute she gazed back at him, inhibition and desire warring within her. He was giving her a choice. There would be no seduction; the compulsion must be mutual. As she wavered, he made a sudden movement to turn from her. Her doubts dissolved and her decision was made for her. Quickly catching his hand with her left one, she laid it back upon her breast.

'I don't want you to leave,' she said huskily, her body tensing as she waited for his possible rejection.

'You know what will happen if I don't?' he warned her. Wordlessly, she nodded. His free hand moved around her, sliding down her spine to splay over the firm roundness of her buttocks. As he eased her closer to him, mindful of her injured arm, he said, 'It's not too late to tell me to go. If I stay, I'll make you mine.'

The tension drained from her limbs; her body turned to liquid as she leaned against him. She was his. Her heart, her soul was already in his keeping. 'I am yours,' she whispered, raising her face to his, her lips parted softly to receive his kiss.

He didn't deny her. His mouth covered hers in a warm, tender caress, teasing her lips, stoking the flames of desire. His head moved to permit his lips to explore the smooth contours of her face as he breathed in the scent of her, savouring her taste. With the tip of his tongue, he traced a circle in the pink shell of her

ear. 'Let's go to your bedroom.' Without waiting for
her assent, he lifted her from her feet and carried her
into the next room.

The satin bedspread was cool and firm beneath her
heated body when he lay her down upon it. For a
silent moment he stood over her, drinking in the
beauty of her supine form. A frown touched his
forehead as his eyes rested on her bandaged arm.
'Maybe this isn't such a good idea. I don't want to
cause any damage.'

In answer, Allie sat up, reaching out with her good
hand to fumble with the buttons of his shirt. 'You
won't hurt me . . . unless you leave.'

His hand captured hers, briefly pressing it against
his chest where she could feel the heavy pounding of
his heartbeat. 'I'd hurt myself more.' Letting her hand
fall, Allie watched him strip the shirt from his hard,
muscled torso, then shed the rest of his clothes.

Slowly and with care, he lay down beside her, his
hand stroking her velvet flesh, his fingers moving to
explore the intimate recesses of her body. Her left
hand made its own excursions, testing the hard nub of
his male nipple, burying itself in the carpet of his
chest hair.

The rhythm of their love-play quickened as ardour
built to a hard, aching need. The languid petting
changed to urgent and demanding caresses, until at
last Linc moved over her, spreading her thighs to
receive him. Breathless seconds ticked by as he stared
down into her eyes, probing their grey depths. She
might have only imagined that words of love were
torn from his lips as he plunged deep inside her.
Perhaps it was only an echo of her own thoughts and
emotions.

*   *   *

Dissatisfied by what she saw, Allie studied her reflection in the mirror, knowing that it was getting too late to do anything about it. If she had been going to slice up her arm, why couldn't she have done it to her left one instead of the one she relied on all the time? It had taken several tries to apply her make-up before she'd managed to get it on relatively smudge-free. And the contortions she'd gone through getting into this sundress didn't bear thinking about.

However, peering at herself critically, she guessed she didn't look that bad. Her nap had washed away the shadows from beneath her eyes, so she didn't really need any more make-up than the touch of eye-shadow and lipstick she'd been able to manage. Her dress was pretty and feminine, a cotton floral print with a full skirt and strapless neckline.

If only the effect didn't have to be destroyed by this ugly sling! Grimacing, she glared down at it, tempted to dispense with it for the evening. However, the faint ache in her arm warned her she would be pressing her luck if she did. The afternoon's lovemaking had left it a little sore.

A secret smile tugged at Allie's lips. Even if her arm fell off as a result of her exertions, the intimacies she'd shared with Linc would still have been worth it.

Linc wasn't in the living-room when she entered. She had heard the phone ring as she'd walked along the hallway from her bedroom, and concluded that he must have answered it in his study.

For several minutes, she wandered about the room, taking in the view from the windows, checking out Linc's bookcase. She felt nervous, if the truth were known. Did he feel the same as she did about this afternoon? They hadn't talked much afterwards. Spent, they had lain in one another's arms in a gentle cocoon of fulfilment. Finally, Linc had roused himself, leaving her to dress for dinner.

Did he see their interlude as a beginning, the start of a commitment, the way she did? Or was it just a moment of passion to him, a moment never to be repeated? How would he greet her when he joined her?

Suddenly unsure, Allie took the coward's way out by delaying the moment of meeting. Removing herself from the living-room, she went to the kitchen. After all, she *did* owe Mrs Dorcus an apology for sleeping through lunch.

The kitchen was a haven of homey warmth and tantalising smells. Given the newness of the house, Allie was expecting to find a modern, laboratory atmosphere in the food preparation area, but the large kitchen had a delightfully old-fashioned air, for all its modern equipment. Huge beams hung with copper pans and antique china crossed the ceiling. Braided rugs dotted the unglazed tile flooring set out in a cobblestone pattern. Gingham curtains fluttered in the open windows, and a large deal table covered in oilcloth dominated the centre of the room.

The housekeeper was standing at a large, modern stove as she transferred fried chicken from a well-seasoned cast-iron frying pan to a platter sitting on the marble counter-top. She turned on hearing Allie enter, her expression questioning.

'I just wanted to tell you I hope I didn't put you out too much by missing lunch,' Allie said. She sensed something off-putting in the older woman's manner and felt her cheeks growing warm. Did the housekeeper know what had gone on between Linc and herself this afternoon and disapprove? On the other hand, the woman had never been the soul of friendliness in Allie's previous encounters with her, so perhaps it was just her manner.

'It was no trouble. I expect you needed a rest,' Mrs Dorcus replied, turning back to her cooking. 'Dinner will be ready soon.' Her tone was laced with dismissal.

Allie knew she should leave, but was compelled to stay watching none the less. It was fascinating. The only fried chicken Allie had ever encountered was the sort that came in a cardboard box with the picture of a southern gentleman on the front of it. It was amazing to think that Mrs Dorcus had taken one of those naked things from the shop and turned it into that platter of crisp, mouth-watering morsels.

Having removed the chicken, the housekeeper added flour to the pan and began whisking it around with the fat. When it was bubbling nicely, she added water from the pot of potatoes boiling on the back burner to the roux.

As she stirred the mixture, she caught sight of Allie still standing by the table. Her glance was faintly hostile and the girl flushed. 'I'm sorry, I didn't mean to get in your way. I was just watching you make gravy.'

'I don't do fancy sauces. I'm just a plain cook,' she responded defiantly, taking Allie's explanation as criticism.

'But you're very good,' Allie said sincerely. 'The casserole you served the other night was delicious.' The older woman didn't look mollified, and a sense of helpless desperation washed through Allie. She appeared to have offended Linc's housekeeper in some way, and he wouldn't thank her for that. In these times, it couldn't have been easy for him to find someone to take care of the house and Jason for him.

Somehow, she didn't think it had anything to do with her and Linc being together earlier either. As the housekeeper turned away, her back rigid with affront, Allie decided the only thing to do was to beat a hasty retreat. 'I'm sorry if you don't like anyone watching you cook. I . . . I don't cook much and was just wanting to see how you make gravy. I've never tried it.'

Before Allie could turn to leave, Mrs Dorcus stayed her. 'You don't make gravy?' she asked, sounding appalled. 'What do you do?'

'Sometimes I buy the kind that comes in cans,' Allie admitted. 'Mostly . . . well, I eat a lot of TV dinners.'

The older woman snorted. She couldn't have looked more horrified if Allie had told her she dined on tinned dog food every night. 'Don't you know how to cook?' she asked.

Chagrined, Allie shook her head. She'd never had an opportunity to learn. Her childhood had been spent mostly in institutions, boarding-schools and college dormitories. The kitchen staff in those places wouldn't have welcomed a child hanging about wanting to learn how to cook.

'You can't do much with your arm like that, but you can watch me if you want to. Come over here,' Mrs Dorcus ordered gruffly. Despite the harshness of her tone, there was an underlying warmth that had been missing up until now.

'You saw me put the flour in?' she asked as Allie joined her in front of the stove. 'Make sure you've got plenty of fat, then you let it bubble, stirring it to work out the lumps. Next, you add . . .'

CHAPTER EIGHT

ALLIE thoroughly enjoyed her impromptu cooking lesson. Mrs Dorcus turned out to be an excellent teacher, with a vast store of patience when answering Allie's questions. Like most highly intelligent people, Allie had never been content with simple explanations. It was all well and good for the cookbook to tell you not to over-mix your baking powder biscuits, but Allie wanted to know why . . . and how could you tell when they were mixed enough but not too much?

Fortunately, Linc's housekeeper appeared to know the answer to these and all Allie's million other questions and, more importantly, didn't resent her asking them. When Linc discovered them together nearly half an hour later, the two were deep into a discussion of the qualities of whipping cream, and how it could be used to produce butter.

He stood watching for several minutes, until Mrs Dorcus looked up and saw him standing by the door. She glanced over to the kitchen clock, then hurriedly got up from the table where she and Allie had been having their discussion. Wiping her hands on her apron, she said, 'I'd better put the vegetables on to cook. I expect you're wanting dinner soon.'

'I'm in no hurry. I was looking for Allie to see if she wanted to join me for a drink before we eat.' He stood looking at the two women, a curious half-smile on his lips. 'What were you doing?'

Allie rose and walked over to him. 'Frances was just giving me a few cooking tips.' His straight dark brows lifted at Allie's use of the housekeeper's Christian name. The older woman had worked for him for several years, and she'd never invited *him* to drop the formal Mrs Dorcus!

Allie gave him an uncertain look. It occurred to her that the housekeeper was his employee, and he might not appreciate her coming into the kitchen and bothering her. She wasn't the mistress of his house, and she hoped he didn't think she was trying to usurp that role just because of what had happened between them earlier. 'I hope you don't mind,' she said meekly.

'No, of course not,' he assured her. His smile took on a mocking tilt. 'She's a brave woman, though. I probably should offer her danger pay.'

It took a moment for Allie to catch his drift. Then she remembered the incident in Clare's kitchen with the salad dressing. She gave Linc a hurt look and encountered his deep blue eyes, sparkling with devilment. A smile started to replace the frowning set of her mouth as a sense of humour she didn't know she possessed took over. The sight of Linc 'dressed' in oil and vinegar *had* been rather funny.

When his deep male chuckle rang out, she found laughter bubbling up in her own throat. He slid his arm around her shoulders companionably, giving them a friendly squeeze. 'How about having that drink with me? It's my turn to have a share of your company.'

Allie absolutely loved the possessive way he had said *that*! Linc's arm didn't drop from around her until they had reached the living-room. When he released her to go and fix the drinks, Allie's eyes followed him with loving adoration. She almost felt like pinching herself, to see if this was a dream. Linc was everything she—any woman—could want in a man. Strong and sexy, he was intelligent, witty, kind . . . and she loved him. Even more, she felt in her heart that he loved her as well.

Rejoining her, Linc handed her the glass of orange juice she'd requested. 'Honestly, I was quite surprised to find you in the kitchen with Mrs Dorcus. She's usually a real bear when anyone invades her domain.'

'She didn't seem too pleased to see me when I first went in,' Allie admitted. 'She was really nice to me after the first few minutes, though.'

'I'm glad you get on so well, since you're going to be staying for a while. She and Elaine are usually at daggers drawn. Elaine won't even set foot in the kitchen when she's there, because Mrs Dorcus has turfed her out so many times.'

Finding her glass of great interest, Allie wished he hadn't brought up Elaine. She preferred not to even think about the other woman in his life. Not that she was that sure Elaine was the other woman in his life. It could very well be that she was just a friend of Linc's and the rumours Allie had heard were just that—rumours. Linc seemed to have too much character to be the sort of man to start an affair with one woman while heavily involved with another.

Glancing at him through her lashes as she took a sip of her juice, Allie was sure that he just wouldn't do it. There was too much integrity written in the lines of his decisive features and direct dark blue eyes for him to be a rake.

Feeling happier, Allie permitted herself a tiny, smug smile. Even if Elaine wasn't her rival, it was none the less ego-satisfying to know that the other woman didn't get along with Linc's housekeeper, while she and Frances had hit it off like a house on fire.

Recalling those first few minutes she'd spent in the housekeeper's company, Allie didn't need any of her college degrees to figure out why the woman didn't think much of Elaine, either. Frances had told her she was a 'plain cook' who didn't do 'fancy sauces'. It wasn't hard to imagine Elaine with her art deco fruit salad sweeping into the kitchen and trying to take over. Allie didn't blame Frances for chucking her out. No one wanted to be around a person who made them feel inadequate or inferior.

Not that Mrs Dorcus need ever feel that way about her cooking. When they sat down to dinner a little while later, Allie decided that the chicken looked just as delicious on her plate as it had in the kitchen. As she had missed lunch, Allie felt more than able to do justice to the crispy chicken, mashed potatoes with gravy and new peas and carrots the housekeeper had prepared. She was only going to save enough room for some of that strawberry shortcake she'd watched Frances make for dessert!

Her plate loaded, Allie sampled the vegetables, then glanced over to Linc. His knife and fork were poised over a succulent piece of breast meat as he prepared to cut off a bite. She looked down at her own plate and the drumstick reposing on it. With her arm in a sling, she couldn't wield a knife and fork if her life depended on it. She had hoped that they were going to consider the chicken finger-food. Although, taking in the lovely china and linen tablecloth that graced the table, that would be rather incongruous.

'Is anything wrong?' Linc asked suddenly, noticing her expression. 'Your arm? This afternoon . . . your stitches didn't get torn out, did they?'

'No . . . no, I'm fine.' Looking down at her plate to hide the flush of heightened senses brought about by his reference to their afternoon's lovemaking, Allie said quickly, 'Everything certainly looks delicious.' Taking up a forkful of the potatoes, she shoved it in her mouth while she decided how she was going to ask him to cut her meat for her. It was embarrassing, and made her feel like such a baby—especially when she wanted him to see her as all woman.

He didn't say anything for a moment, then suddenly set his knife and fork aside. 'You know, Mrs Dorcus's fried chicken's just about my favourite food.' Using his hands, he picked up the breast piece and bit into it. After chewing, he swallowed and set the piece back on his plate. Licking the grease from his fingertips with obvious enjoyment, he said, 'It's messier this way, but for some reason it always tastes better if you eat it with your fingers.'

Allie stared at him doubtfully for a moment, then saw one of his eyelids drop in a slow wink. She grinned back at him, then picked up her drumstick with her left hand and took a big bite from it. It tasted heavenly.

The meal passed in an atmosphere of relaxed congeniality. It was so relaxed, in fact, that when their easy conversation hit a perilous stretch as they lingered over coffee, Allie nearly blundered. Up until now, she hadn't had to take many pains to conceal the level of her intelligence from Linc. Fate had given her more than a generous helping hand in that direction! Linc seemed to catch her out in the most idiotic situations, and she knew he thought she was a bit dim, to say the least.

Consequently, she wasn't expecting him to speak of his work on anything more than a superficial level.

The conversation had been flowing smoothly in shallow channels. Suddenly, though, Allie felt as if she were navigating rapids, and one error would swamp the fragile relationship with Linc.

It started simply enough, with his explaining his daily routine. 'I expect you'll still be asleep when I leave in the morning. I plan my day to get over to my office on the mainland early so I don't get back too late in the afternoon. Jason gets back from school around three, so I try not to be too much later than that.'

'I knew you left early. I've heard the plane leave.'

'Sorry, do I wake you up?'

Allie shook her head. 'I'm an early riser.'

Linc reached across the table and picked up her left hand. Stroking the back of it with his thumb, he looked intently into her eyes. 'Then we have something in common,' he said softly.

Warm, fluid sensation flowed from the gentle touch of his hand, arousing sleeping desires. Speechless, she stared back at him. She could have drowned in the pools of his deep, deep blue eyes.

The moment passed, though, and he released her hand to sit back in his chair and take a sip from his coffee-cup. 'Unfortunately, I haven't been able to get home very early from work lately. We've been really busy.'

'You do somthing with computers, don't you?' Allie asked, although she knew the answer.

'That's right. We started out custom-fitting existing software packages for individual businesses, but more and more we're getting into the development of our own programs.'

Allie nodded, her interest caught. 'It must be very interesting.' She looked down at her lap, not wanting him to see just how keen her interest was. She knew that program development was interesting. It was what *she* did, and she found it fascinating!

'It is, although I don't do that much programming myself these days. Most of my time is spent on administration. I do have one baby I'm keeping to myself.' He leaned towards her, his elbow resting on the table. His eyes were fired with enthusiasm. 'Some fellows came in a couple of months ago—sunken treasure hunters. They've developed a new type of echo-sounder for mapping the ocean floor, and want my company to work up the program to read the data it produces. With this new equipment they're hoping to get a much more detailed picture of what's down there.'

Despite herself, Allie looked up at him, questions burning on the tip of her tongue. It was the echo-sounder that did it. The tie-in with her own pet project was obvious. Could a parallel application be to use it to count fish—to get a more detailed read-out? With better data, could she . . .

She braked her thoughts ruthlessly, almost choking on the words she'd been about to speak. Linc was watching her with disturbing alertness. Although she knew her comments couldn't be of the least importance to him, she sensed he was waiting for them with unnatural intensity.

And she'd been almost ready to give the game away! Earlier this self-same evening she had been thinking how Elaine had earned Frances's enmity by being a know-it-all. And here she was, almost ready to make the same mistake as the other woman.

Men did not like intelligent women! Particularly when they competed in the same field as themselves!

She shrugged slightly, giving what she hoped was

an apologetic but flirtatious smile. 'I'm afraid you lost me somewhere back at the software level. That sounds as if you make cuddly sweaters.' As the keen light faded from his eyes, Allie rushed on, 'That was a super meal. Maybe I should clear the table for Frances. I expect she wants to get the kitchen cleaned up for the day and relax.'

Hastily crumpling her napkin, she set it beside her plate and stood up. Linc said, 'You don't have to bother. You're a guest.'

Although he protested, there was a certain flatness to Linc's voice. Rattled by her near slip, Allie barely noticed. 'I don't mind helping,' she assured him, starting to gather up the used dishes. She wanted to get away from him for a few minutes. The enjoyment in their evening together had temporarily gone stale, and she needed a few minutes away to regain her equilibrium.

Allie lingered in the kitchen, helping Frances to load the dishwasher and put away the leftover food. When she finally went back to Linc, he was standing in the living-room, moodily staring out across the water. He turned at her entrance, and although he smiled at her she sensed a certain reserve in him, a faint withdrawal.

She could have kicked herself. He'd told her she was a guest, but she'd ignored him. He was probably annoyed by her presumption in making herself at home in his housekeeper's kitchen.

'I hope you didn't get tired of waiting for me,' she offered tentatively. 'I . . . er . . . Frances seemed to have quite a bit of cleaning up, so I helped her. I hope you don't mind.'

'No, of course not,' Linc said, looking surprised.

'You don't have to apologise. It was great of you to pitch in . . . Mrs Dorcus has a lot to do every day, and it's nice for her to have some help for a change.'

He sounded totally sincere, and yet Allie still sensed a faint reserve in him. Although she didn't really think that was the problem, she mentally vowed to decline Frances's offer to give her a few cooking lessons while she was staying here. In future, she'd stay out of the kitchen. It would be better to remember she was a guest, and not risk appearing as though she was trying to entrench herself into Linc's household.

A few minutes later, Allie admitted that somehow the companionable atmosphere between them had dissipated. She had declined Linc's offer of an after-dinner drink and seated herself in a chair near the fireplace. When he had his brandy, Linc came to stand near her, his elbow resting on the mantelpiece.

Although they chatted, the conversation was sluggish, marred by long periods of silence. With one finger, Allie traced the squares on the chess-board set on the end-table by her. She wished she could turn back the clock, find some way of recapturing their earlier rapport. She didn't know what to say or do, where to begin.

'Do you play chess?'

Startled from her unhappy thoughts by Linc's sudden question, Allie answered automatically, 'Yes.' Of course, that wasn't what she should have said at all. She knew it as soon as she noted Linc's surprise, as well as the keen light that suddenly shone in his dark eyes. With the uneasy strain in their relationship since dinner, the last thing she wanted was for him to find out how she had been deceiving him about the level of her intelligence.

'Let's have a game, then,' he suggested, setting his glass aside. Before she could stop him, he pulled the end-table with the chess-set on it around to the front of her. Next, he brought another easy chair over for himself, and sat down across from her.

Dismayed, Allie stared down at the board. Why had she ever said she played? The 'yes' had leapt from her tongue before she knew what had happened. It was like having the minister to lunch and suddenly spouting swear words you never realised you knew, just to afford the Fates a laugh.

'When I said I played, I didn't really mean it.' On seeing Linc's frown, she amended, 'I mean, I've only played a few times . . . a long time ago. I barely know which pieces are which.'

He sat silently for a moment, then his jaw muscle suddenly firmed. He said in an oddly determined tone, 'Let's give it a try. I'll make allowances for you and help you with your game. You can start. Do you remember which are the pawns and how they move?'

Reluctantly, Allie nodded and randomly pushed one of her light jade pawns forward one space. She was going to hate this. Temperamentally, she wasn't geared to doing less than her best, and she was a very good, very competitive chess-player. To pretend she was a rank beginner so that Linc wouldn't discover just how good she was was going to be one of the most unsatisfying charades she'd had to undertake since embarking on the role of the dumb blonde.

'You know you could have moved that pawn forward two spaces, because this is the first time you've moved it?' Linc asked her, studying the board.

'I forgot,' Allie lied, shoving the pawn forward another square.

Linc nodded, then moved one of his own

pawns forward.

The play continued for another forty-five minutes. Linc was really being very patient and kind, but Allie was nearing the point of screaming in irritation and frustration. It had been different when Frances was showing her how to cook—for one thing, she didn't know how to cook! She did know how to play chess, though, but she dared not protest when she disagreed with Linc's advice or congratulate him when he made an astute move. Whenever he pointed out a glaring error on her part, she was forced to clench her teeth to hold back telling him that she knew very well what she had done. His constructive criticism was driving her mad!

It wasn't really fair to him—however, Linc appeared to be a very fine player and she was dying to pit herself against him in a genuine contest of skill.

She knew she should probably excuse herself and go off to bed before she said or did something stupid and gave herself away. Unfortunately, temptation loomed at that moment. Allie surveyed the board. Her light green forces had been seriously diminished, while Linc's dark men gained control of the board. However, she could see that by sacrificing her remaining rook, she could achieve a checkmate in six moves.

Recklessly, she pushed the rook four squares forward and captured one of Linc's pawns.

He studied her move for a few seconds, then looked up at her. 'Are you sure that's what you want to do?'

She nodded, unknowingly wearing a faintly smug smile.

He cut it off with a glare of exasperation. 'Allie, haven't you learned anything from what I've been telling you?' he demanded, his patience run out. 'You have to think ahead in this game and keep an eye on where my men are! Look what you want to do. You're going to lose your rook if you go ahead with this move, and all you'll have to show for it is a lousy pawn. My knight is sitting right here ready to take your piece.'

'I know that,' Allie retorted, stung by his curt tones, her own patience gone. If he was tired of her apparent denseness, well, tough! She was sick *and* tired of the condescending advice. 'That's the move I want to make!'

'Umph,' he snorted, giving the board a disgusted look. 'This obviously wasn't a very good idea.' He reached beside him and picked up one of the pieces he had previously captured and started to set it back on the board.

'What are you doing?' she demanded, catching his hand so he couldn't place the piece. 'Aren't we going to finish?'

'I am finished!' Pulling his hand free, he set the knight in its place with a decided clunk.

Incensed, Allie didn't consider her next words, 'You only want to quit because I was on my way to winning!'

Linc treated her to a scathing look, his eyebrows lifting. 'Don't kid yourself, honey. I don't know if you just don't want to learn or you can't. Whatever, there was no way you were going to beat me, so stop being a poor sport!'

Allie opened her mouth to argue further, then shut it with a snap. She didn't know whether she wanted to curse or cry. It was only natural for Linc to think she couldn't defeat him. Until that last move, she'd either pushed the pieces at random or deliberately erred. He couldn't be expected to know that that last play had been the start of a trap for his king several moves later.

In a way, his ending the game was a lucky escape for her. Had it continued, she *would* have checkmated him. How would she have explained it? She didn't want him to guess at her expertise, to know that she was smarter than she'd led him to believe. She'd had a lucky escape all right, so why wasn't she feeling relieved? Why did she feel resentful?

In a rather ominous silence, Linc returned his easy chair to its original position and moved the chess-table back to the side of Allie's chair. When he'd finished, he walked back to the fireplace and glanced rather pointedly at his watch. 'It's gone ten o'clock.'

It was hardly a subtle hint, but Allie wasn't going to ignore it. Their time together had gone sour, and she could do with an excuse to escape. Rising to her feet, she gave Linc a terse smile, 'If it's that late, I think that I'll be on my way to bed. Goodnight.'

'Goodnight,' he echoed briefly. She felt him watching her as she walked from the room. Earlier that evening, she hadn't really expected that she'd be going to bed alone tonight. When she walked from this room, down the hall, she'd pictured him beside her, his arm around her waist.

However, Linc was making no move to accompany her. She was glad about that, she told herself. She wasn't in the mood for lovemaking. She didn't want his arms around her; she didn't want his kisses. She didn't want him to come after her . . . did she?

CHAPTER NINE

ALLIE spent most of the next day ensconced on Linc's veranda with a fashion magazine. Although she tried to work up some enthusiasm for the illustrations, it wasn't easy. A lot of women went into raptures over the idea of fur coats and silk dresses, but Allie wasn't so sure she liked the idea of wearing the skins of dead animals and the secretions of worms.

She wished Linc hadn't buried himself in his study. They should talk things out. The atmosphere when they had met at breakfast had been decidedly frosty. She'd tried to bring their disagreement out into the open, she really had. She knew she had been unreasonable when Linc had cut their chess-game short the night before. Her apology had been met with one from Linc. He'd apologised for losing his patience.

But their mutual expressions of regret hadn't seemed to make much difference. They were still uncomfortable with each other. It was odd, really. Allie sensed that Linc honestly wanted to make up with her, that he disliked the strain between them as much as she did. Something was holding him back, though, and as a result he was making a conscious effort to keep a barrier between them.

Allie was a brilliant problem solver. Her work didn't involve just sitting before a computer punching in commands. She analysed, probed, and sometimes worried over the snags that arose. Once she discovered the root cause of the difficulty, with innovation and imagination she would devise a solution.

But her relationship with Linc wasn't a mathematical algorithm, it wasn't a computer program. She couldn't think the 'bugs' out of it. She couldn't even figure out exactly what it was that was wrong.

Or did she know what was wrong and didn't want to admit it? She had dismissed Elaine as a rival, and yet, could it be that thoughts of the other woman were causing Linc to back off? If Linc was committed to Elaine, in love with her, his conscience must be giving him hell right now. In a moment of transient passion, had he betrayed the woman he really loved? He *wasn't* the philandering type, and he would bitterly regret what had happened between himself and Allie.

The sound of a car drawing up to the house broke into Allie's musings. She glanced at her watch, then cast her magazine aside and got up from the lounger. It was probably Jason's grandparents bringing him back from his weekend with them. Maybe with Jason's return things would improve between her and Linc, she thought, then hastily tempered the idea. There was no point in indulging in delusions. It was perhaps more realistic to view the return of Linc's boisterous son as providing her with an excuse to cut short her stay.

Linc had emerged from his study when Allie went into the house. He was standing in the foyer talking with an older couple as his son stood scuffing the toe of his shoe against the tile flooring. They broke off their discussion when Allie joined them, and Linc quickly made the introductions.

'Jean and Alvin, this is Allie Smith. She's staying

here for a few days to recuperate from an accident. Allie, these are my in-laws, Jean and Alvin Delaine.'

As she shook hands with the couple, Allie wondered what Jason's grandparents thought about their son-in-law's having a young woman staying at the house. However, she soon realised that they were paying scant attention to her.

The formalities out of the way, Mr Delaine turned back to Linc to continue with their discussion. His florid complexion was rather flushed, and there was a hard look in his pale blue eyes. 'What's this nonsense Jason's been telling me about you hauling him over to Vancouver to see some headshrinker?' He reached down and tousled his grandchild's hair. 'Jason is a perfectly normal little boy. He's just high-spirited, and all this cock-and-bull his teachers have been laying on you is just that! If they knew how to do their jobs, there wouldn't be any problem. And as for his being——'

'Excuse me a moment, Alvin,' Linc cut him off. 'I think that my son has already eavesdropped on too many discussions.' He looked over to Allie. 'Would you mind taking Jason to his room and keeping him company while he unpacks his suitcase?'

'Certainly,' Allie agreed, smiling down at the little boy and holding out her hand to him. In a way, she wished she could stay. She hadn't known that Linc was seeking professional help for Jason. She knew the child was a handful, but she hadn't realised his problems were that serious.

Jason's response to her overture was a rather sulky glare, but at a curt order from his father he accompanied Allie down the hallway to his room, dragging his weekend case behind him.

'I wanted to hear what they were going to say,'

Jason grumbled, when Allie closed the door after they'd entered the room. 'They were talking about *me.*'

'Well, yes,' she admitted. 'But you need to get unpacked now.' Using her uninjured arm, she lifted the suitcase on to his single bed and opened the lid. Lying atop the jumble of clothes was a mutilated starfish with one tentacle missing. It had obviously died recently, and the stench of rotting fish wafted up at her. 'Jason, what have you got this in here for?' Allie grimaced, making a face at the smell. It was enough to make her sick. Gingerly, she picked out the mangled rock creature with her thumb and forefinger, and held it away from her. 'Bring me the wastebasket.'

'You can't throw it away!' Jason protested. 'It's my spearmint. It's going to grow a new leg!'

Allie looked over to the little boy, then back at the dead starfish. 'I don't think so.'

'But it will. On TV they showed starfishes grow new legs after they lost one. I cut the leg off this one so I could see it for myself,' he said earnestly.

'I think it only works with live ones, honey,' Allie explained. 'This one is dead.' Was it ever dead!

'Is it really dead?' Jason asked. He moved closer and peered at the object in her hand. 'It was wriggling when I cut its leg off yesterday.'

'Well, it's dead now,' Allie said rather grimly. Poor starfish. From the looks of it, Jason hadn't taken its tentacle off with surgical precision. It was pretty hacked up. 'Could you get me the wastebasket so we can get rid of it?' The smell was making her stomach queasy. She glanced over to Jason's open suitcase. Mrs Dorcus was probably going to have to throw out his clothes.

'But we don't want to do that! Let's have a . . . ah . . . an ah-auta . . .'

'An autopsy?' Allie supplied automatically.

'That's the word. Can we?'

Allie wrinkled her nose, then shook her head. 'It smells too bad.'

Jason screwed up his nose as well. 'It does, doesn't it?'

'So let's get rid of it.' This time, Jason brought over the tin wastecan to her and let her drop the dead creature into it. 'You'll have to take it outside in a few minutes or it will smell up the whole house.'

'OK,' he said agreeably, then asked, 'Can I go down to the beach and see if I can find another starfish?'

'No!'

'But this one died. I didn't get to have my spearmint.'

'Jason, it died because you cut its leg off,' Allie told him, although stuffing it into his suitcase probably hadn't done anything to prolong its life. 'You can't just keep making poor starfish suffer because you want to play some silly game.'

He treated her to an affronted look. 'It wasn't a silly game. I was being a scientist. Scientists do spearmints.'

From what she had overheard of Linc's conversation with Jason's grandfather, she gathered the child had trouble with his teachers. She could well believe it. He might not be much of a scientist, but he certainly was a darn good debater. It was impossible to keep one step ahead of him. He had a reply to everything.

Wishing she knew more about children, Allie finally said, 'Well, maybe you'll just have to come up with some kind of experiment you can do without having to murder any more starfish.'

Her choice of words wasn't the most fortunate. The little boy's mouth began to quiver as he looked down into the wastebasket. 'I didn't mean to *murder* it,' Jason whispered in a slightly awed tone. 'I just wanted to see it grow a new leg.'

Recalling that the child seemed to be overly influenced by the television programmes he watched, Allie wondered if he was expecting the police to come looking for him at any moment. 'I know you didn't mean to hurt it,' Allie assured him heartily. 'It was only a starfish, after all. Now, just set the wastebasket over by the door for the time being, and you can take it outside later. We'll read a story or something while your dad finishes talking to your grandparents.'

Jason moved the waste-container, but his mouth was set in a determined line when he came back to her. 'I don't like stories. I told you that before.'

He certainly looked like his father when he wore that intractable expression! Allie glanced over to the bookcase by the window. For a kid who didn't like stories, he was well endowed with books. On closer study, though, most of them looked as though they had never been opened. Looking back at Jason somewhat helplessly, Allie wondered what she was going to do with him if they didn't read. She didn't know very much about entertaining children. Linc wouldn't want her to let him go back into the main part of the house, though, when he was trying to have a serious discussion with the boy's grandparents.

Jason himself supplied the answer. Going to the bookcase, he removed a dog-eared tome from the lower shelf and handed it to her. 'You can read me some of this.'

Allie turned it around to read the title, then looked

up at Jason. 'Are you sure this is what you want?' She
gestured to the bookcase. 'There are lots of nice books
there. Why don't we pick one of them? *The Wind in
the Willows* might be nice.'

'I want this one. That other book is stupid. Moles
don't talk and live in houses!'

He had a point there. Resigned, Allie seated herself
on the side of the bed with the book in her lap. Jason
was six or seven years old, and it was odd to say the
least that his favourite book happened to be an old
college text on natural history. However, when it fell
open naturally to a specific section, she began to
understand. A ferocious looking *Tyrannosaurus Rex*
stared up from the page at her. Not content with just
the picture, Jason prompted her and Allie began to
read the dry, technical narrative to the apparently
fascinated little boy. His eyes stayed on her in rapt
attention as she stumbled over the long, unfamiliar
words, only interrupting occasionally to correct her
when she mispronounced one!

Linc's entry into the bedroom about thirty minutes
later interrupted them, and rather thankfully Allie set
the book aside. She felt as if she'd been saying tongue-
twisters for hours.

'Your grandparents are going to be leaving in a few
minutes, so you should come out now to say goodbye
and thank them for having you,' Linc addressed his
son. His gaze moved over the room, landing on the
open suitcase resting at the foot of the bed. 'I thought
that I told you to unpack!'

Standing up, Allie started to explain, 'I thought he
should leave it for a while.' Before she could tell him
that she wanted Mrs Dorcus to check out the contents
of the suitcase to decide whether the dead fish smell
could be washed out of Jason's clothes, or they should

just be burned, Linc interrupted her with a sarcastic glare.

'Thanks a lot, Allie. Just what Jason needs is somebody to encourage him to ignore my instructions!' He held his hand out to the boy and motioned him out of the room. 'What's that awful smell?' he asked the child as they left.

Allie glared at the doorway they had disappeared through. She felt like picking up the wastebasket and throwing that damn dead starfish at him. He could have at least given her a chance to explain! Still angry, she stalked from the room and went to her own bedroom, closing the door behind her with a decided snap. She had barely met the Delaines, so hopefully they weren't expecting her to come say farewell.

Once in her room, Allie pulled her suitcase from the bottom of the wardrobe where Mrs Dorcus had stowed it. Using her good left hand, she began to awkwardly stuff her clothes into it. That rotting starfish was a rather appropriate send-off, she thought bitterly. There was an old saying about fish and guests going stale before too long. Linc's whole attitude today had made it very clear that she had outstayed her welcome.

She didn't hear the knock on the door when it came. Swearing under her breath as she wrestled with the suitcase to get it closed, she was concentrating on her anger so that the hurt didn't overwhelm her. She wasn't being very successful either, because tears were seeping down her cheeks.

When she didn't answer, Linc entered the room anyway. Out of the corner of her eye, Allie caught him watching her and turned to confront him. 'What are you doing in my room?' she demanded belligerently, dashing the tears from her face with her left hand.

He stared back at her briefly, his eyes narrowing in a frown as he took in her tears. 'I was wondering where you were. I thought you would come out to say goodbye to Jason's grandparents.'

'I didn't feel like it,' Allie sniped petulantly, then muttered defensively, 'I barely met them.' As Linc stepped towards her, she turned her back to him. When she'd taken her hand off the top of the suitcase, the lid had sprung open and some of her clothes had escaped. She picked up a blouse, and blindly jammed it back in.

From behind her, Linc said, 'Look, I'm sorry about what happened in Jason's room. He explained about the starfish.'

Allie didn't respond, but kept her rigidly unyielding back to him. After several seconds of taut silence, Linc continued, 'Look, I know I was unfair. I was upset, not with you but with Alvin. We don't get on very well, and we had a pretty trying discussion. I shouldn't have taken it out on you, and I apologise.'

Allie swallowed hard against the lump in her throat. Why was she so helpless at staying angry with Linc? Instead of yelling at him and telling him where he could stick his apology, all she wanted to do was cry.

When he rested his hands on her shoulders, she tried ineffectually to shrug them off. Tightening his grip, he forced her to turn and face him. The tears were streaming from her eyes and a sob caught in her chest as she bit on her lower lip to stem the tide of emotion.

'Oh, damn, Allie,' Linc groaned, gathering her to his strong, hard chest. One hand firmly against her back, he lifted the other to gently stroke the smooth silk of her blonde hair as she wept against him. 'I never wanted to hurt you,' he murmured. 'Please believe me, it was the last thing I wanted to happen.'

The womblike comfort of his embrace had a calming effect on her shattered composure, but her voice was still choked with tears as she muttered against his breast, 'You were so rotten today.'

'I know, I know,' he agreed contritely. Moving his hand from her nape, he brought it around to lift her face to his. For a moment he stared down into her tear-soaked eyes, then he kissed the salty moisture from her lashes. 'I'm so sorry, Allie,' he whispered against her lips.

His mouth was warm and loving against her own, a kiss of comfort and regret. It dried the remaining tears in her sad grey eyes and stilled the sobbing in her breast. The caress lasted only a few moments, then he cradled her head against his shoulder, holding her securely in his embrace.

The action calmed the riot of her emotions, leaving her spent but tranquil. His gentle kiss, more than any demand of passion could have, had told her that he loved her. And, as long as he loved her, nothing else mattered.

When he eased her away from him, her eyes shone up at him, sparkling with stars of love. He met her gaze, his dark eyes sober and strangely wistful. 'Don't leave yet, Allie,' he asked roughly, glancing to the suitcase on the bed behind them. 'At least let me take care of you until your arms heals.'

She stared back at him, moistening her lips with the tip of her tongue. He could take care of her forever. Her heart was forever in his keeping already. He had no need to ask, and yet he waited for her answer. She nodded slowly.

For several long moments he looked down into her face. Then suddenly he swooped, kissing her long and hard with a passionate, painful urgency. It was a harsh, unrelenting kiss, but she revelled in it. There was a sense of desperation in his touch that communicated itself to her, sparking the need to reassure him. Her hand sought his shoulder, the nape of his neck, holding him to her. She pressed against him, wordlessly giving herself to him.

He responded, his mouth savouring hers, draining it of all she offered. Finally, though, Linc lifted his head, and there was something disturbingly final in the gesture. 'Thank you for staying,' he said thickly.

Removing her arm from about his neck, then letting his arms drop to his side, he stepped back a pace. He seemed to be composing himself, drawing himself inwards and pushing the last few minutes behind him. When he spoke, it was of the prosaic. 'Dinner will be ready in about an hour. I have it a little earlier when Jason is around,' he informed her. 'You might rest until then, clean up a bit.' His hand reached out to stroke her still damp cheek. As his fingertips touched the wetness of her cheek, though, he quickly pulled back, as though regretting his action. 'I'll see you later,' he said abruptly, turning away and striding from the room.

There was a bittersweet happiness to the next few days, ruled by the drone of Linc's float-plane. He left very early in the morning, signalling to the rest of the household that it was time for them to stir. Allie was usually awake before he left, but some inner reticence held her back from seeing him off. Instead, she'd wait for the sound of the plane leaving before rising from her bed.

She breakfasted in the kitchen with Frances and Jason, chatting with the housekeeper and coaxing

Linc's son to finish his meal. School wouldn't be out for the summer vacation for another two weeks, so afterwards she helped Jason to dress and walked him to the stop where the school bus picked him up.

Her working day began then. Going to her own cabin, she spent the day with Harold developing her fish-count project. It was slow going, as she could use only one hand on the keyboard, but that didn't bother her. Usually, she was an impatient, though meticulous worker, but that sense of inner urgency that usually accompanied a new project didn't develop. She enjoyed her work, but was not chained to it. In some ways it was just a time-filler until Linc and Jason returned.

Promptly at two-thirty, Allie shut down the computer and tidied away her notes. Strolling to the bus stop, she only had to wait a few minutes for the big orange school bus to arrive, and with it, Jason.

As they walked home Jason chattered away about his day in school, but when they reached the top of the drive leading to Linc's house they always fell silent. After a few minutes, they were rewarded by the distant drone of the float-plane, a sound that sent Jason galloping down the driveway and around the house to the seaplane dock.

Linc had been wonderful in including her in his afternoons with Jason. There had been games and outings with the little boy. One afternoon, he'd taken them in his boat over to Brother XII's island. On another, they'd gone into Nanaimo and lain on the sand at Departure Bay beach while Jason built sandcastles near the water's edge.

Their afternoons together were relaxed and happy. Linc teased her and his son, slipping his arm around Allie in a companionable fashion as they strolled

along. When she'd fallen asleep at the beach, he'd
woken her with a gentle kiss, his lips brushing lightly
over hers. They had stared into one another's eyes for
a long, unspeakable moment, before Jason had run up
to them, demanding that they come and inspect his
last construction project. As they got up, brushing the
sand from their clothes, their eyes met in a moment of
wry amusement. A warm flood of happiness washed
over Allie. It was so easy to pretend that she was the
mother in their family group—that Linc was her
husband.

After an early dinner with the little boy, the
atmosphere changed subtly. Relaxed and easy in her
company while his son was present, Linc seemed to
withdraw once his son was tucked away in bed. It was
as though an invisible shield dropped between them.
They drank coffee together, chatting about the day's
events, but it wasn't long before Linc would excuse
himself to go to his study. Allie wouldn't see him
again until the next afternoon.

On Thursday afternoon, Allie glanced down at the
white bandage on her arm as she and Jason walked
silently to the house, listening for the sound of the
plane. That morning, Clare, temporarily free of
house-guests, had driven her into town to see the
doctor about her arm. The wound was healing nicely,
and he replaced the heavy bandaging with a lighter
covering and let her dispense with the sling. Although
he didn't want to remove her stitches for another few
days, he told her that if she was careful she could start
using her right hand to some extent.

There really wasn't much reason for her to continue
staying at Linc's.

The scar on her wrist probably would be the only
tangible reminder she would have left of these last few

days. She hadn't had a chance to take any of her birth-control pills before Linc had made love to her, but there had been no consequences. It was the time of the month that she should start taking them now, but it seemed rather pointless.

Maybe Linc really was that busy, his job so demanding that he needed to devote every evening to working in his study. But often the light in her room would still be on when he finished. She could hear his footfalls as he moved along the hall to his own bedroom. He never paused at her door. He never came in.

'I wonder where Daddy is,' Jason said, breaking into her thoughts.

Allie glanced over to him and saw his frown. She realised they had nearly reached the house and still hadn't heard Linc's plane coming into land yet.

'I expect he was delayed taking off,' she reassured the little boy, though a frown was starting to pleat her forehead as well. Although he was only a few minutes late, she couldn't help worrying. Linc was always so punctual, and small planes were rather dangerous. It seemed as if one was always hearing about one that had crashed.

'Oh, damn!'

'Jason!' Allie admonished in a shocked voice. 'That is no way for a nice little boy to talk. I know you're disappointed about your father, and . . .'

'I wasn't saying it because of Daddy. Look!' He pointed to a car pulled up before the front door. 'That's Auntie Elaine's car.'

'Oh,' Allie said, Jason's 'damn' echoing in her own mind. Elaine hadn't been over since Allie had been staying at Linc's—a circumstance Allie had been exceedingly grateful for. Confused as she was about the other woman's place in Linc's life, she simply didn't want to see her. She was too fearful that a meeting just might confirm some of the worst of her fears.

'I don't like her,' Jason confided as they walked on to the house, their steps unconsciously dragging.

'You shouldn't say things like that,' Allie chastened half-heartedly. She and Linc's son had apparently found something else they had in common.

The front door of the house opened and Elaine emerged, pausing a few moments on the step to have a word with Mrs Dorcus. Reluctantly, Allie and Jason went to join them.

CHAPTER TEN

WHEN Elaine turned away from the front door and suddenly caught sight of them, Allie saw her look of disconcertment, before she managed to assemble a polite smile for her and Jason. As they reached the step, Frances winked from behind Elaine's back and quickly disappeared into the house. Coward, thought Allie, knowing the housekeeper's opinion of Elaine. Left on her own, she prepared her own smile of greeting for the woman.

'Allie, how are you feeling? Linc told me about your accident.'

'I'm fine. My arm's healing well.'

The other woman's gaze lingered on Allie's bandaged wrist. 'I can see that must be. From the way Linc spoke, I'd imagined you swathed in bandages from head to toe. I'm glad to see it wasn't all that serious.'

Was Elaine implying that Allie was purposely using her injury as an excuse to stay with Linc? she asked herself, immediately on the defensive.

'I just saw the doctor today. He put on a smaller bandage and told me I didn't have to wear a sling any more,' Allie explained sharply.

'I'm sure it must have been very painful when it first happened,' Elaine offered quickly, looking slightly cowed by Allie's tone. 'I'll bet you're relieved it's healed so quickly and you'll be able to get back to your own place quite soon.'

There was no mistaking the hopeful inflection in Elaine's voice. Allie met the other woman's spaniel eyes and read the unhappiness in them. She suddenly felt sorry for her, and a little guilty because she knew she was the source of that unhappiness. She'd wasted a lot of time being jealous of Elaine, resenting her relationship with Linc, but she had a great deal of empathy for the woman's feelings at this moment. Elaine suspected something was going on between Linc and herself, and it was tearing her apart.

'And how are you, Jason?' Elaine asked suddenly, avoiding Allie's gaze by turning her attention to the little boy. 'I guess you're looking forward to school breaking up for the summer. You'll have to come and spend a day with me then.'

Jason glowered back at her. 'Don't want to,' he muttered. With the agility of a tadpole evading a predator, he slid past the two women on the porch and through the door into the house.

Elaine shot his retreating back an embarrassed look. 'Linc is really going to have to do something about that child. He's unbearably rude,' she muttered.

Allie wished that she could get away with being as rude as Jason, and scoot off into the house as well. Instead, politeness demanded that she spend a few more uncomfortable minutes with Elaine's unwelcome company.

'Well, I must be running along,' Elaine said finally, her face still faintly flushed from Linc's son's rebuff. 'I stopped in to have a word with Linc, but I guess he isn't going to be home until much later. I'll call him . . . we're very good friends, you know,' she added in a rush of bravado.

'I'm sure you are,' Allie said gently. Poor Elaine, she thought, pensively watching the other woman as

she walked to her car. There was something faintly
pathetic about her boast of friendship with Linc. Linc
had once mentioned that Elaine had a hard time
making friends. It was easy to believe. She wasn't a
very likeable woman.

And Elaine had talked of Linc's soft-heartedness.
He seemed to be the older woman's only friend.
Maybe pity played a large role in that friendship.

Linc arrived home around eight o'clock in a mood
that Allie had never seen him in before. Over the last
few days, she'd come to learn he had a fairly equable
disposition, albeit occasionally moody, so seeing him
in a good mood was nothing new. However, the
description 'good mood' hardly did justice to his high
spirits that evening.

He came bounding up the outside stairs from the
float-plane dock and swept into the house like a
hurricane. A grin was splitting his face when he strode
into the living-room demanding to know where
everyone was.

'Frances went into Nanaimo to see a movie with one
of her friends, and Jason's in bed,' Allie explained,
eyeing Linc curiously. Although he couldn't know the
housekeeper was gone, the woman usually kept to
herself in the evenings after dinner was finished. As
for his son, Linc knew very well that Jason's bedtime
was seven o'clock.

'Jason's asleep?' Linc asked, looking slightly
deflated.

She nodded, hoping he wasn't planning to wake the
boy. At the best of times, Jason wasn't the easiest lad
to persuade to sleep, and without his father or Mrs
Dorcus to back her up Allie had had quite a tussle
getting him into bed on time. He'd only stopped

asking for drinks of water, toilet visits and all the other little procrastinating tricks he knew about fifteen minutes ago. It would be a crime to wake him and start it all up again.

Linc didn't, though. Instead, his grin reappearing with a flavour of mischief, he walked over to her. Catching her around the waist, he swung her off her feet in a wide circle. When he set her back down, he planted a hard kiss on her astonished lips, then laughed down into her face. 'I guess it all falls on your shoulders to help me celebrate, then!'

'Celebrate?' Allie asked. His bubbling spirits were infectious and, although she didn't know their source, she couldn't help laughing with him. 'What are we celebrating?'

'No, wait,' Linc ordered, raising his hand imperiously. He went over to the drinks cabinet and, rummaging around in the built-in fridge, finally came up with a half-bottle of chilled champagne. Holding it up for her to see, he said, 'We definitely need to drink a toast to this!' He turned around to retrieve glasses, asking, 'Did Mrs Dorcus leave me anything to eat? I didn't have a chance earlier and I'm starving.' Glasses in hand, he turned back giving her a self-mocking smile. 'I'd better have something with the champagne or I'll be too muddled to tell you my news.'

'She left some cold meats and salads in the fridge,' Allie informed him. 'I can get you a meal.'

'Will you join me?'

Allie hesitated only a moment before nodding. She'd eaten earlier with Jason, but her appetite hadn't been up to much—probably because Linc had been absent. She could eat again now that he was here.

Linc's arm about her waist, they walked together to the kitchen. As they entered the room, she asked

'Won't you tell me what's happened while I get dinner put together?'

He halted, causing her to stop walking as well. His look was considering, then a gleam of devilry entered his eyes. 'Not yet. I'll tell you while we eat. You get the food out of the fridge and I'll go set the table in the dining-room.'

She gave him a sour look that he only laughed at. In retaliation, she poked him in the ribs with her elbow and he winced in exaggerated pain. 'Just for that, I'll keep you dangling a little longer,' he said maliciously. 'I order you to go and put on your prettiest dress.' He treated her to a hauty sneer down the length of his nose, but his grin suddenly destroyed the pose. 'I need a shower, anyway.' Firmly turning her by the shoulders, he pointed her in the direction of her bedroom and gave her a little shove. 'Fifteen minutes.'

It was closer to a half an hour before Allie left her bedroom to return to the kitchen wearing a floaty chiffon cocktail dress in delicate spring green. She'd taken extra care with her appearance; Linc's celebratory mood had been catching.

Sharing a meal in the dining-room with Linc would make tonight special as well. They usually ate in the kitchen with Jason and Mrs Dorcus. Allie enjoyed the practice because it made her feel a part of Linc's family. However, dining alone with him definitely had its attractions.

Linc was at the refrigerator taking out the bowls of salads and plate of cold cuts Mrs Dorcus had prepared earlier. He paused in his task when Allie entered the room. For several moments, they stared silently at one another. Linc's hair was still damp from the shower and it gleamed in the evening sunlight streaming through the window. He'd changed from his business suit into dark trousers with a matching navy turtleneck sweater that clung to his torso like a second skin. He looked handsome and so virile that Allie felt slightly weak in the knees just looking at him.

The bodice of Allie's dress fell in soft folds with a plunging V-neckline and, if it wasn't her prettiest dress, it was at any rate her sexiest. It certainly had more to recommend it than the jeans and top she'd been wearing when Linc came home. She didn't have to ruin the effect by wearing that awful sling, either.

He whistled at her, giving his approval to her appearance, then frowned slightly. 'Shouldn't you be wearing your sling?'

She had somewhat mixed feelings about her recovery. Naturally, she was glad that her arm was so much better, but, when it was, she had no real reason to continue staying in Linc's home. She didn't want that thought intruding on this evening, though. Perhaps it would be their last together.

Smiling back at him, Allie shook her head. Making her tone purposely light, she said, 'You're not the only one with something to celebrate. I saw the doctor today and he said I didn't have to wear it any more. I can even start using my hand again if I'm careful.' She held up her right hand and wiggled the fingers for him to see.

Linc closed the space between them in two long strides. Catching up her bandaged hand, he gently brushed the backs of her fingers with his lips. 'Then we have a doubly good reason for celebrating.' He looked deep into her eyes, suddenly serious. 'I really am glad you're better. I was worried about your arm. I was afraid I might have set things back, done some damage, that afternoon we made love.'

Drowning in the midnight-blue of his eyes, Allie shook her head. Emotion choked her throat so her voice was a bare whisper, 'You didn't.' His words melted the doubts she'd harboured these past few days. They explained so much. She had worried when he hadn't made love to her again, had seemed to be rejecting her. She'd wondered if she'd failed him somehow, had been inadequate.

He'd only been worrying about her injury, though! That first afternoon, passion had caught them both unawares. They'd been swept away by it and unable to give thought to anything but their all-consuming desire. That was probably why Linc seemed to withdraw from her whenever they were alone, as well. He didn't want to allow that need they had for one another to gain free rein and risk hurting her.

His mouth came down to cover hers in a warm, gentle kiss, laced with a thread of promise. His lips stroked hers, then her cheeks and eyelids. He lifted his head and his arms briefly tightened around her. 'First things first, my love. Let's go and eat.'

Together, they finished loading the food from the refrigerator on to the trolley to push it into the dining-room. Linc had been busy in that room while Allie had been changing. He'd drawn the curtains against the evening sunlight, casting the room into shadow, then illuminating it with candles. Their light danced over the gleaming china and silver, sparkling off the champagne glasses.

While Linc opened the wine, Allie filled their plates from the trolley and took her place at his right hand. When their glasses were filled, Linc lifted his to her, saying, 'My first toast is to you. To your health and happiness.' He drank deeply of the wine, his eyes holding hers over the rim of his glass. There was promise in his gaze, an avowal.

After a moment, he lowered his glass and reached out to top it up from the champagne bottle. 'And now, so as not to keep you in suspense any longer, I'll make my second toast.' He raised his glass, saying, 'To my son, Jason.'

'Jason,' Allie echoed, taking a sip of her wine. When the glasses had been returned to the table, she asked, 'So what's happened with Jason?'

Folding his arms on the table, Linc looked over her, the lines fanning out from the edges of his eyes crinkling with happiness. 'It seems that that little brat of mine has been hiding his light under a bushel, as they say. It's turned out that he is a certified genius!'

Allie blinked at him. 'He's what?'

'A genius! A little Einstein! I had a meeting with a psychologist this afternoon. He did some tests on Jason and has discovered he has an IQ of a hundred and seventy-four.'

He was beaming at Allie, but she found it difficult to smile back at him. Linc was so obviously pleased, and yet, from her own experience, she wasn't that sure that he should be. Certainly, high intelligence was a gift, but it could also be a tremendous burden. Labels such as 'genius' especially could sometimes make it even harder to carry.

'Is it such a shock?' Linc asked. Looking slightly deflated by her lukewarm reaction, he picked up his fork and started to eat.

Realising her response wasn't exactly what he'd been hoping for, Allie said, 'Well, I'm stunned.' He slid her an offended look, so she amended hastily, 'I mean, I did realise that Jason's very bright, but . . . did you take him to the psychologist because you suspected something like this?'

Linc shook his head, and he was smiling again when he looked up from his plate. 'Just the opposite, in fact. That's what makes this news such a relief! You see, Jason has been having a terrible time in school this year—disruptive in class, not doing his work, back-talking the teacher. I've been called in to see her so many times in the past few months, it's a wonder people don't think we're having an affair or something. Anyway, things came to a head a few weeks ago.'

His smile vanished and a grim set replaced it on his mouth. 'Actually, I think it was that day you ran out of petrol. I'd been to see not only Jason's teacher, but his principal and counsellor as well. There seemed to be no doubt that he was going to fail grade one, and they felt that he might have some kind of learning disability. They were feeling me out about putting him in a special class next year for children who are mentally slow.'

'I can't see where they came up with that,' Allie exclaimed. 'I mean . . . just look at his favourite book, that one about dinosaurs! Even *I* have a hard time understanding it.'

A shadow seemed to pass across Linc's eyes as she caught his gaze. Perhaps it was only a trick of the light, but it brought her up short as she realised what she had said. She would have to watch her words more carefully. Now wasn't the time for making revelations of her own. She knew parents loved basking in the reflected glory of their brilliant offspring—her own were prime examples—but most men didn't feel that same way about the women in their lives. Superior intelligence in women was too much of a threat to their egos.

However, she was also vitally aware of how

important it was that she discuss this with Linc. She *knew* exactly what Jason was saddled with if he indeed was as bright as his father had been led to believe. Linc would need to give the child a great deal of care and understanding if Jason was to exploit his gift to the fullest without its becoming a curse.

Linc grew serious as he continued. 'I admit I didn't want to accept their assessment, either—that's why I took Jason to see a professional psychologist over in Vancouver. That was the basis of my disagreement with Alvin the other day,' he explained as a side-note, although Allie had already guessed that.

'But I still don't understand how his teacher could have been so off-base.'

'Partly, I think she isn't as good at her job as she could be, but Jason himself has to shoulder some of the blame. You know how he is—strong-willed, stubborn, but more than anything he loves to be the centre of attention. He misbehaved and disrupted the class because he's bored. Regular schoolwork just doesn't have any challenge for him. I also think he discovered somewhere along the line that by not doing it, by pretending he couldn't do it, he's got a lot of special attention and help from his teacher.'

They lapsed into silence and gave their attention to the meal before them. Allie glanced over to Linc from time to time. A little smile played about his mouth, although he was pensive as well. She wished she could have been more enthusiastic about his news. Trying to make amends, she said eventually, 'It really is good news. I know how pleased you are.'

'I am,' he agreed, returning his attention to her. 'It's kind of scary, too. It'll mean a lot of changes in our lives.'

'Changes?'

'Well, of course. The psychologist offered a few suggestions. He feels that Jason would really benefit from an enrichment programme. I'll have to arrange something.'

'I see.' Allie's appetite had fled and she pushed an errant piece of lettuce around her plate with her fork. She felt disturbed and vaguely uneasy. Virtually her whole life had been an 'enrichment programme', and yet it had never made her particularly happy.

'I suppose the school district will be able to advise you,' she offered when Linc didn't continue. 'They usually have special programmes for extraordinary cases.'

In the candlelight, she saw Linc's jaw clench and his voice was harsh. 'I don't know if they do, but I don't think I want Jason to continue his education here. I think you can understand why I'm not too impressed by the local school, with all this happening. No, I'm afraid Jason will have to go away to school.'

'Go away?' Allie echoed. 'You mean you'll be moving back to Vancouver?' It would be such a shame to take Jason back to the city after having lived in this lovely rural home. There was so much for a growing boy to do here: boating, fishing, beach-combing, tramping through the woods.

'The school the psychologist recommends is in Montreal. I'm afraid Jason will have to board, since my business is here.' He caught her expression and misinterpreted it. 'Don't worry, I'm not going to sell this place. We can still use it for holidays, although I'll probably get a small apartment for myself over on the mainland.'

'You can't send Jason half-way across the country to boarding-school!' Allie objected, appalled. 'He's just a little boy. What about the friends he has here? What about you and Frances? He'll be miserable.'

'Of course he won't!' Linc denied, a tinge of anger colouring his tones. 'Naturally, it'll be something of an adjustment at first, but once he's established it will be the best thing for him. He'll be with other children like himself, kids he can relate to. More importantly, though, he'll find challenge and interest in learning and can direct his energies towards that instead of being the class hooligan. He'll be happier!' he concluded forcefully.

Allie stared at him. 'Who are you trying to convince—me or yourself?'

'You,' he retorted with only the briefest hesitation. 'But I don't know why I'm bothering. It is really none of your business what arrangements I make for my son's education.'

That hurt, and Allie winced from the blow. Her face was pale as she regarded him, damming tears behind the smoke-grey of her eyes. 'Maybe that's true,' she admitted huskily. 'But I think you'll be making a mistake if you send Jason away from you.'

With dismissive deliberation, Linc looked away from her and casually picked up his wineglass. He swallowed the last dregs of wine, then reached out for the champagne bottle to refill his glass.

Anger getting the best of her, Allie caught his arm. Arrogantly, he looked down at her fingers gripping the sleeve of his sweater, then met her eyes. 'Listen to me, Linc!' she demanded. 'I know what I'm talking about. I was sent away to school, a "special" school so I would be with my intellectual peers. I hated it!'

'There isn't a comparison,' Linc asserted, brushing her hand off his sleeve, and pouring the last of the wine into his glass. 'That would have been an entirely different situation.'

'It was the same damn situation—exactly!' she told him hotly.

He held her eyes momentarily; they were hard and implacable. They didn't soften when he suddenly laughed, not very pleasantly. 'Start being realistic, Allie. It isn't the same. Learning will come easy for Jason when he's in the proper circumstances. I'm sorry if you had a hard time when you were in school, but you can't compare your experiences with those that Jason will have. My son's a genius.' He savoured the word, his eyes derisive as they caught hers. *She* was no genius, they said. 'It would be irresponsible for me as his father not to give him every opportunity to develop the intellect that God saw fit to bestow on him.'

Allie knew that he had misunderstood her when she'd told him about going away to school. He thought that the special school she'd talked about had been for children of low intelligence. However, would it really do her any good to correct his misunderstanding? She studied his face. It was set in granite and his demeanour was just as hard. He'd made his mind up and she could see that nothing was going to change it.

Nevertheless, she made one final attempt. 'But does that mean he *has* to be sent away?'

'In this case, it does.' Pointedly ending the discussion, he crumpled his napkin and placed it beside his plate. 'Would you like some coffee?'

Allie hesitated only briefly. 'Yes, I'll go and make us some.' Hastily scrambling up from her seat, she left the room. He didn't try to stop her.

She took as long as she dared over the coffee-making, analysing what had happened between them. She felt so confused and unhappy. Was the argument her fault? Had she been butting in, offering advice, when really it was none of her business? Yet, how could she just have stood by without saying anything when the man she loved was heading for such a disastrous decision? Over the last few days, she'd grown to love Jason as well as his father. She didn't want him hurt, and they would both be hurt if Linc sent Jason to Montreal. Jason needed his father close to him, not half a country away.

And Linc . . . didn't he need his son with him, too?

When at last she could tarry no longer, Allie placed the coffee things on a tray and carried it into the dining-room. She paused for a moment by the door. Linc had left the table. He'd opened the curtains and was standing by the window, staring morosely out across the water.

It broke her heart to be at odds with him. She hadn't meant to apologise when she'd left the kitchen. In her heart, she felt she was right about Jason's future, but she couldn't live with Linc's being angry with her.

Linc turned and saw her standing by the door. Immediately, Allie came all the way into the room and set the tray at the end of the table.

'I wanted to apologise for butting in,' she said, keeping her eyes down as she set out the coffee-cups. 'You're right. It's none of my business and you are Jason's father, so it's up to you to decide his future.'

'Don't worry about it,' Linc said flatly, coming up beside her to help himself to the coffee. 'You're entitled to your opinion.' There was rebuff in his voice, and the way he turned away from her to go back to stand at the window made Allie's heart sink. She could have saved her breath. He wasn't interested in her apology.

Taking up her own cup of coffee, she seated herself

at the table with it. Silence swirled about them, oppressive and smothering.

After a few minutes, Linc turned back to face her. Leaning against the window, he said conversationally, 'I see your arm really is much better.'

Allie shrugged—the conventional words of a polite host. He was going to pretend their argument had never happened. 'It is. I didn't even think about it when I carried the tray in.' She concentrated on stirring her coffee, although as she hadn't added cream or sugar it was a totally unnecessary occupation.

'Yes, you seem quite capable of looking after yourself again.'

Only a few heartbeats passed before she looked up, but in that space she knew the blood had drained from her face. Her hands felt cold and clammy, the chill spreading to her heart. She had to swallow before she could speak. 'I guess I am. Maybe I should move back to my own place.'

Linc didn't say a word, but his eyes held her. She thought she saw a curious shadow cross over them, bleak and filled with sadness. But when she blinked that look was gone and his navy eyes were blank and unreadable.

He broke off the look first, concentrating his attention on his coffee-cup. 'That would probably be a good idea,' he said, casually lifting his cup to his lips and taking a sip of the dark brew it contained.

'Yes,' she said, her voice barely above a whisper. She cleared her throat and said stiffly, 'Perhaps I should go tonight.'

Linc afforded her a patronising smile, gesturing to the scene outside the window behind him. 'Don't be silly. The sun's nearly set and it will be dark soon.'

Allie bit her lower lip, then in sudden decision pushed her coffee-cup away and stood up. 'I might as well pack up tonight, at any rate,' she announced.

'Suit yourself.' He shrugged his indifference and turned his back to her to gaze out of the window once more.

Swamped by bewilderment, Allie stood where she was for several moments, staring at the broad expanse of his back. It couldn't just finish like this. Any moment now, Linc would turn around and smile at her, tell her that he had only been teasing. They had disagreed, but surely that wasn't enough to cause him to send her away?

'I really am sorry if you think I spoke out of turn about Jason,' she said suddenly, desperately. Silence greeted her. It was as if she'd never spoken. Hot tears filled her eyes as she stared at the man she loved. With one last throw of the dice, she whispered roughly, 'I love you, Linc.'

He started, then slowly turned around. His face was a savage mask of anger. In a low, harsh voice, he said scathingly, 'Get out of here, Allie. This is the end of it, so just leave me alone!'

CHAPTER ELEVEN

ALLIE carefully steered the Pontiac into the drive and drew it to a halt before the closed garage doors. For a moment, she sat regarding the substantial brick house that was the Smiths' family home. Her last bolt-hole, she thought bitterly. She would have to be very careful of the men she met while staying here. She'd no place left to run when things turned sour.

As she got out of the car, though, she didn't think she would be in any danger. Kevin had bruised her heart, but Linc had shattered it. It was going to take a long time to fit the pieces back together again. Even when it mended, if it mended, she didn't think she'd ever meet anyone she could offer it to with the same intense love with which she had offered it to Linc.

A wave of despair washed over her, and she had to pause on her way to the front door to overcome it before moving on. She hadn't spoken to him since the night they had argued about Jason's future. She'd spent that night lying sleepless in her bed, waiting. She'd been so sure that it was all a mistake, that he'd come to her, accepting her apologies, making everything all right again.

He hadn't come, though. She'd fallen into a heavy slumber around dawn and, when she'd awoken, he and the float-plane were gone. Mrs Dorcus had been in the kitchen when she'd emerged from her bedroom. Linc had already told his housekeeper that Allie

was moving back to the cabin that day. There hadn'
been much she could do but gather her thing:
together and return to her own home.

That night, though, she'd planned to see him, t
talk to him, to see if there wasn't some way back. Th
float-plane had returned in the afternoon, but sh
wanted to give him time with Jason, time to settle i
after work, time to settle her own nerves. In the early
evening, before setting out for his house, she'd gon
up to the loft just to check that his plane was stil
there.

It had been, that and his boat. And Linc had beer
standing at the corner of the veranda staring ou
across the Strait. There had been something
disconsolate in the stance of that solitary figure, and
hope had risen within Allie. He was missing her
regretting their argument, the same as she was.

Before she could turn from the window to go to
him, another figure joined his. He slipped his arm
about Elaine's waist and together they stood at the
railing, Linc's hand lifting as he pointed ou
something to the woman.

Allie felt an eerie sensation of *déjà vu* creep over her
Another night, Linc had stood at that railing, his arm
around a woman. He'd talked of Brother XII, the mar
who was irresistible to women. Mrs Dorcus had tolc
her more of the story. He was a man who'd romanced
many of his feminine disciples, but, when he sailec
away for good, had taken with him the one womar
who'd been the constant figure in his life. She'd beer
known as Madame Zee, a theatrical alias that soundec
as though she'd picked it out of a cheap paperback
mystery. However, she'd been his right-hand, staying
in the background throughout all his peccadilloes, bu
knowing whom he would always come back to ir

the end.

Allie had packed to leave that night and driven away the next morning. Coward that she was, she'd written a note for Clare, thanking her for the domestic equipment she'd lent her and apologising for leaving without seeing her. She couldn't have met with her friend again. Clare would have probed and pried, demanded some explanation for Allie's precipitate departure. After her affair with Kevin, Allie had wanted to spill out her unhappiness and disappointment, to purge herself of the experience. Talking wouldn't ease the pain of the wound to her heart this time, though. It was too deep and too shattered to probe.

The front door opened before Allie reached it. Laura Smith emerged and with quick, light steps came down the walk to meet her daughter. She was a tall, slender woman, with an air of grace and sophistication. Skilful tinting had kept her hair the same shade of blonde she'd had in her youth, the hair colour she'd passed on to her daughter. Her eyes, though, were a clear, pale blue, unlike Allie's grey ones, and her facial features were less refined.

'Allie!' she exclaimed, coming to a halt in front of the younger woman. She made a tentative movement with her arms, as though to embrace the girl.

Allie looked back at her, instinctively withdrawing from the gesture. 'Hello, Mother,' she said quietly.

Laura Smith's arms dropped to her side. 'Your father and I were so surprised when you called this morning to say you were coming,' she said with forced heartiness. Taking Allie's weekend bag from her, she started back up the walk at her daughter's side. 'You've hurt your hand,' she exclaimed, sliding a glance down at Allie's bandaged arm.

Allie gestured dismissively with her injured arm.
She'd nursed and favoured it all during the long drive
across the country, so it wasn't bothering her.
Fortunately, her car had power steering with an
automatic transmission, so it hadn't been that difficult
to drive mostly left-handed.

Her mother was still curious. 'Is that why you're
taking some time off from the Institute?'

The question reminded Allie that she hadn't been in
touch with her parents since giving up her job. It
seemed like years ago. She felt a stab of guilt, but then
reminded herself that they weren't all that close
anyway. She'd only come here now because she
couldn't think of anywhere else to go.

'I left my job at the Institute several weeks ago. I
went out west to see Clare for a while,' Allie explained
when they had entered the house. That was a rather
cryptic way of summing up the last few weeks, but she
couldn't bear to go into greater detail.

'Clare . . . that girl you were so friendly with during
college?'

Allie nodded.

'So you've left your job?' Mrs Smith mused, her
curiosity evident. She set down the luggage by the
foot of the stairs leading to the bedroom floor and
turned to face Allie. Her fine brow was pleated with a
frown of puzzlement, questions hovering on the tip of
her tongue. However, on seeing her daughter's closed
expression, she asked instead, 'Have you had lunch?'

Allie shrugged. She was too depressed to be
sociable, and just wanted to hide in her room and lick
her wounds in private. 'I'm not hungry. I'm a little
tired, though. I'd like to go up to my room and rest for
a while.'

'Yes, of course, you've had a long drive.' Allie had

only the briefest glimpse of her expression before her mother turned to pick up the case again to carry it upstairs. Surprise intruded into her state of lethargic despondency. Her mother seemed hurt that she wanted to escape from her company so soon after her arrival. She wouldn't have thought it mattered. If anything, the Smiths had spent so many years shipping her off to boarding-schools and camps that Allie would have thought her mother would be relieved she wasn't planning to linger underfoot.

'I guess I wouldn't mind a cup of coffee before I go up,' Allie suggested, still not really sure that she had read her mother's expression correctly.

Mrs Smith was smiling when she turned back, her pleasure so obvious that Allie knew that she *had* been hurt. 'I'll put the pot on. Do you want to wait in the living-room while I get it set up in the kitchen?'

Instinctively, Allie moved to agree to the suggestion, then checked the impulse. It would give her a few minutes to herself, but suddenly Allie realised how selfish that would be. Her mother seemed so genuinely glad to see her. Smiling at her parent, she said, 'Let me come with you. A friend . . . a friend was going to teach me to cook.' Allie's voice caught at the memory of Linc's housekeeper, and she had to swallow to clear it before she could continue. 'You always make such good coffee. Maybe you can show me how you do it. Whenever I make perked coffee it tastes awful. I've ended up relying on instant.' She slipped her arm through her mother's and gave it a slight squeeze.

If surprised by her daughter's unexpected demonstrativeness, Mrs Smith was also delighted. Her own arm tightened, drawing Allie closer to her side. 'Why, of course I'll show you how I make coffee, dear. In fact, I can teach you to cook while you're here. I never realised you wanted to learn.'

It was peaceful sitting in the kitchen drinking coffee with her mother. They weren't totally at ease with one another, but as they chatted about inconsequential topics Allie realised that the despair she'd lived with since leaving Vancouver Island had relented somewhat. Deep inside her, she knew there would always be a hard ache whenever she thought of Linc. As she relaxed in her mother's company, though, she felt more able to cope with it and able to go on living.

'I'm surprised to hear you left your job at the Institute. I thought you were very happy with it. I hope things didn't go wrong for you,' Mrs Smith said eventually. She didn't look at Allie, but concentrated on stirring her coffee.

'It was time for a change,' Allie hedged. Despite the warmth that was creeping into their relationship, she wasn't ready to impart confidences.

There was a slight tension in the silence that followed, and Allie realised that it emanated from her mother. She asked, 'Is anything wrong?'

'No, no,' Mrs Smith said quickly. 'I just . . . well, I guess you know your father and I never wanted you to take that job in the first place.'

'Yes, I do know,' Allie replied coldly, her jaw muscles tightening as she went on the defensive. 'You wanted me to take that job with the University of Toronto.'

Hostility crackled in the air, and Allie saw her mother nibble her lower lip. Finally she said quietly, 'I don't think you understood our reasoning. It seemed as if we'd missed your whole growing up, what with you always away at school. It was worth it of course,' she avowed fervently, her very passion

almost suggesting that she harboured some doubt.
'You had the kind of education that someone of your
potential deserved. But . . . well, of course we missed
you. When you left university, we sort of hoped you'd
find a job closer to home . . . like the one at the
University of Toronto. You could have lived at home
and we could have got to know each other.'

'I see,' Allie murmured. She'd never thought of it
like that. Her parents' home was located in a suburb
of Toronto, and if she had got a job in that city's
university she could have lived with them. She hadn't
thought that they wanted her, though. She wished her
mother had told her this back then, but there had been
other considerations, too. 'I know Henning is a long
way away, but the job was more what I wanted.
Besides, the Institute has some of the best minds in
the country working there. I wanted to learn from
them by working with them.'

'Oh, I know all that. It's a real brain trust, but your
father and I wondered if maybe you might not have
been happier at the university, where the students at
least would have been more of your generation. You
didn't have much of an opportunity to mingle with
your peers when you were a child. I dare say all those
great brains at the Institute were years older than
yourself. It would have been nice for you to be around
younger people, to date, that kind of thing.'

Allie sat silent, not quite knowing what to say. She
realised that her parents had been more aware of her
problems than she'd known at the time. She'd always
thought it must have been an easy let-out for them to
keep her in the educational programme that they had.
She wasn't so sure now. Maybe they had wanted her
with them, but had thought they were doing what was
best. Unfortunately, she felt it had been the wrong

course. A normal home life and loving parents on hand was far more important than all the 'enriched learning environments' in the world.

There would be no gain in telling her parents that now. They'd made a mistake, they were human. And Linc was going to make the same one with Jason, too, she knew, a lump forming in her throat. She hadn't been able to make him realise that, though.

'That sounds like your father's car,' her mother said, getting up to go look out the window. A few minutes later, he walked into the kitchen. Stopping in the middle of the room, he silently surveyed his daughter for several seconds.

'You're home early, Everest,' Mrs Smith said.

He pulled his glance from Allie to speak to his wife. 'I knew Allie was coming home, so I left work early. I'd hoped to be here when she arrived.'

He looked back at his daughter. Allie could sense the uncertainty in him, the shyness. She sensed that, like her mother, his first instinct was to embrace her, but he feared a rebuff. Realising that that was exactly what she had given her mother as a greeting, she knew she couldn't make the same mistake again.

Quickly getting up from the kitchen table, Allie went to him and put her arms around him. 'Hi, Daddy,' she said huskily. He hugged her hard, and, when he released her, Allie went to her mother. 'I'm sorry about the way I acted when I first came. Let's start over.' Wrapping her arms about the older woman, she whispered mistily, 'Hi, Mom, I'm glad I came home.'

As the months passed, Allie *was* glad that she had come home. Emotionally, it wasn't a particularly easy time for her. Her love for Linc was too intense, too lasting to dismiss—the pain of their estrangement too poignant to purge. However, the loving, caring relationship that grew up between her and her parents helped her through her worst moments and gradually she learned that a life without Linc could still be worth living.

They settled into a comfortable routine and Allie enjoyed her role as the daughter of the house. She didn't go out to work, but her parents organised a den for her and she continued working on her fish-count program and, when it was finished, tackled new projects.

She also learned to cook. It proved to be a more valuable lesson than merely learning her way about the kitchen. She'd always felt bitter about her parents' pride in her academic accomplishments. It had seemed that they basked in her reflected glory, taking credit for her intelligence when it was no more than an accident of birth. However, when they exhibited the same pride, the same pleasure in her first not-quite-successful cake-baking venture, she saw them with a new perspective. They loved her. They would have been just as proud of her had she been a poor student who worked and endeavoured to receive a 'C'.

This new understanding cast a different light on her attitude towards her intelligence, as well. She began to see that part of the reason she'd resented her parents' pride in her brilliance had been because they had drawn attention to her uniqueness. Inside, she knew she had always felt half ashamed of her high IQ. She'd thought it made her a freak, and her seeing herself as one had caused her to live her life accordingly. Her absent-mindedness, her dowdy clothes until Clare had taken her in hand, her failure to learn anything of the world outside her narrow academic field—they were all props for the role she saw herself in. As for the rest of the world, she'd expected people to resent her intelligence, and went out of her way to make sure that they lived up to her expectations.

This new insight was evident when she received an invitation to speak at the annual convention of the National Association of Computer Programmers and Analysts. In the past, she had automatically avoided such engagements, not wanting to be the centre of attention. Gaining the esteem of her colleagues by writing papers for journals as Dr A. Jennings Smith was quite different from actually getting up in front of them and presenting her ideas to them in person.

However, this time she didn't send her regrets as she normally would have. Her parents were very impressed that she had been asked, and couldn't understand her desire to refuse. As they pointed out, it was a great honour to speak at such a gathering. More than that, it probably would be fun and the trip would do her good. The convention was being held in Las Vegas, Nevada, a holiday haven she'd never been to.

It was the latter argument that decided her. She knew her mother and father were worried about her. She'd never been able to bring herself to confide in them about Linc, but they knew something was wrong. She couldn't hide her depression from them completely. It would set their minds to rest somewhat if she took this break.

After the first couple of days, Allie decided that she had been right to come to the convention. She was learning a lot from the lectures, but not half as much as she was from the social times in between them. She'd fallen in with a group of the younger delegates, and they'd been educating her to the ways of black-jack, poker and *chemin de fer*. Some of the lessons were kind of expensive, but the money didn't seem important. They were a cheerful group, none of them serious gamblers, and they laughed whether they won or lost.

Late in the afternoon of the third day, Allie excused herself early from her friends. Gathering up the chips lying in front of her on the black-jack table, she slipped them into her bag. 'I'm going to call it a day,' she announced to no one in particular, turning to slide off her stool.

The man next to her looked up from the cards he'd been studying, saying, 'Stay a while longer. You can't quit when you're winning.' He grinned at her.

Allie made a little face. She had won this afternoon, but then, according to that old saying, lucky at cards, unlucky in love. 'I should be going. I want to go over my notes for tonight.' Her talk was scheduled for that evening's session. Also, she had an appointment with the representative of a software firm beforehand to discuss selling the rights to her fish-count program. Oddly enough, she was more nervous about the latter than of getting up in front of a large crowd and speaking. She'd always been employed for a salary, and this was the first time she'd been faced with selling a program she'd developed on her own. It was rather frightening.

Eric Peterson wasn't going to let her slip away from him that easily, though. Over the last couple of days he'd been quite impressed with Allie Smith, and wasn't going to pass up the opportunity to have her to himself for a while. The fact that she was obviously an expert in his own field was secondary, although he didn't like stupid women. Dove-grey eyes, blonde hair like spun silk and a curvy, sensual figure overrode any considerations for her IQ.

When the dealer laid a king on the three and ten he was holding, he scooped up his remaining chips and gave up his seat at the table to join Allie. That old saying could work both ways. *Un*lucky at cards . . .

'You probably know your speech backwards by now. Let me buy you some dinner,' he suggested, catching up with her a few yards away.

'I couldn't eat,' Allie admitted. 'The butterflies in my stomach would not appreciate it.'

'Then let's just have a drink together,' he persisted.

She shook her head. 'I really want to be on my own for a while. I've had enough of crowds.'

'I wasn't planning to take that lot with us.' He gestured to the other players still at the table. 'I just meant the two of us. Can't you be on your own with me?' he asked teasingly.

'Oh,' Allie said, disconcerted. Eric was one of the half a dozen or so conventioneers that she'd spent time with over the past couple of days. They'd stayed together as a group and she hadn't even thought of him as an individual. She gave him a considering look. He was really quite attractive, big and blond with laughing blue eyes. A specialist lecturer, he was no dummy and had a bright future ahead of him. A lot of girls would be thrilled at his obvious interest. She wished she could be one of them.

Allie shook her head, saying gently, 'I'm sorry. I just want to go to my room and rest. Maybe after my talk?' she suggested, trying to soften the blow. Although it was months since her break with Linc, she still wasn't ready for any kind of involvement with someone else.

'So it will be you, me, and all the rest of them,' he

said, glancing over his shoulder at the group they had just left. He looked back at her, his expression wry, and Allie bit her lip, affording him an apologetic look. 'Oh, well, don't worry about it,' he said. Turning away, he went back to the black-jack table and resumed play.

In the lobby, Allie stepped into the first available lift and pushed the button for the upper floor where her room was located. Unfortunately, it headed down to the parking garages first. She should have been paying attention to the directional arrow before she got in, she thought, chiding herself, but resigned to the delay.

When the lift stopped, Allie moved back into a corner to give whoever was getting on more room. She hoped they weren't just checking in with a ton of luggage. However, the man who stepped in only had a briefcase and a small bag. She glanced up at his profile as the door whispered shut, and suddenly felt as though the lift had plummeted.

'Linc?'

He turned sharply at the sound of his name and looked at her. 'Allie! What are you doing here? Are you on holiday?'

'I . . . er . . .' She shook her head trying to clear it, then reached out and touched his arm. He was real, the tweed of his jacket was rough beneath her fingertips, but still she felt she must be hallucinating.

The door to the lift opened, revealing the lobby. 'Look, I haven't checked in yet. What's your room number? I'll be up as soon as I get sorted out.' He'd dropped his briefcase and his hand came up to cover hers with gentle strength. 'Please, Allie, we have to talk.'

She nodded, still feeling dazed, then mumbled the

number. Linc's eyes searched hers and he squeezed her hand. 'I won't be long.' He dropped his hold on her arm and, picking up his case, strode out of the lift. The door closed and she was alone in the tiny room.

By the time she reached her hotel-room, her brain was functioning again. Linc had said he wanted to talk to her, but did she want to talk to him? Did she want to stir up all the pain and heartache all over again? Yet could she bear not to see him, to snatch this precious opportunity that fate had handed her? She'd by no means got over him. She couldn't even accept an invitation from another man for an innocuous drink, let alone become attached to one.

Before she was half-way through sorting out her feelings about this unexpected encounter, there was a knock at the door. She stared at it from her seat at the edge of the bed. When the summons came again, louder this time, Allie took a deep breath and stood up. Her feet dragging with uncertainty, she walked slowly across the room to admit Linc.

CHAPTER TWELVE

FOR several seconds after she opened the door, they stood mutely staring at one another. There were changes in Linc, Allie noticed. His tan had faded, and there were a few lines around his eyes. He looked as if he'd been working too hard, and there was an aura of strain about him. He'd lost a bit of weight, too. His suit-jacket hung slightly loose over his shoulders.

'Aren't you going to invite me in?' he asked presently.

'Oh, yes, of course,' Allie stammered breathlessly. Even with the changes, he was still heartbreakingly handsome—and she *still* loved him with all the shattered remnants of the heart he'd broken. Gathering her scattered wits, she stood back from the doorway so that he could gain admittance. There was a small sitting-area in the hotel-room, two easy chairs arranged around a table, and Allie gestured him towards it.

When Linc had seated himself, Allie took the chair opposite. She looked down at her hands, at her fingers strangling each other, then out of the window, over to the clock. Anywhere but at Linc.

The silence was loud and oppressive. 'I have an appointment in a few minutes,' Allie blurted out, shattering it. 'What did you want to talk about?' She steeled herself to look at him.

He looked as awkward and uncomfortable as she felt. His eyes caught hers only briefly, before moving to survey the room. 'Nice hotel, isn't it? I'm down here for a computer convention. It started a couple of days ago, but I just managed to get away.'

Surely he hadn't merely come to her room to check out her accommodation! However, he *was* here, and there was something she wanted to know. 'How's Jason settling into his new school?'

With a distracted hand, Linc rubbed the nape of his neck. 'I think you were right about that. He's not happy—that's why I was late getting to this conference. I was in Montreal seeing him. I think I'm going to have to bring him home.'

She didn't know what to say to that, and the quiet of the room settled back over them like a blanket. When she'd thought of Jason, she'd hoped she had been wrong about his being unhappy away from his father and at school. However, finding out that she had been right, she was only glad that Linc had realised his mistake and wasn't going to leave Jason to suffer for it.

'I was wrong about a lot of things,' Linc admitted suddenly, startling Allie out of her contemplation of the carpeting. 'I was wrong to send Jason away to school and was very wrong to send you away. I've missed you, Allie.' Leaning forward in his chair, he reached over and clasped her hand. With one finger, he traced the faint scar running along the side of it and across her wrist. 'I was worried about you, when you left. Clare told me that in your note you'd said you were driving back east to see your parents. I was so afraid something would happen to you, what with your arm not yet healed. It was a stupid thing to do, Allie, running away like that.'

She stared down at his bent head, the dark sheen of his hair. The pain and hurt of the last few months came bubbling up within her and she tugged her hand free. 'I didn't think I had much choice,' she said bitterly. 'You obviously wanted me to leave. You've never bothered getting in touch since.'

He didn't raise his head and she saw his fist clench, the knuckles showing white. 'You're right, of course. It seemed for the best. I couldn't see it working for us.'

'I told you I loved you,' she shot back accusingly. He'd rejected her once, thrown her love back in her face. Did he have to reconfirm that he didn't want just her because they met by chance?

He nodded. 'I know you did. It made it all that much harder to send you away.'

'Then why did you?' she demanded.

He looked up at her, his eyes dark and remorseful. 'It's hard to explain. My first wife, Natalie . . . we had a very old-fashioned kind of relationship. We got married right after I graduated from university—she graduated from high school that year. I went out and brought home the bacon and she stayed at home and kept the home fires burning.' He stood up and walked over to the window, drawing the curtain aside to look out at the city lighting up for the night. 'She was a marvellous cook,' he said half to himself. 'She sewed all her own clothes; had a big vegetable garden every summer and canned and froze all the produce.'

'I see,' Allie muttered when he lapsed into silence again, caught up in his reflections of the past. She saw only too well. Natalie Summerville was about as different from her as another woman could be. Even after all her mother's lessons, she was still only a passable cook. As for those other talents—there was no way. Maybe if Linc had wanted someone who could solve a second-degree differential equation, she would have done. However, she'd never succeed as anyone's image of the perfect housewife. He'd known that, too, so it was no wonder he'd ended their relationship. He wanted a domesticated type . . . someone like Elaine.

Allie afforded him a keen glance. His back was still turned to her. Maybe this was why he'd been so insistent about seeing her. He was a kind man. He'd want to break the news of his marriage to Elaine gently, to try to make her understand his motives.

'I'm already a little late for my appointment,' Allie said briskly, jumping up from her chair. The tears gathering in her throat were nearly choking her, but she managed to keep her voice level. 'I'm afraid I'll have to ask you to leave.'

Linc's head snapped around as she spoke, and he stared at her in confusion, mingled with irritation. 'What do you mean, leave? I haven't even started——'

'I'm asking you to leave. I think you've said everything that's necessary.'

'I——'

'Look, Linc!' Allie cut him off ruthlessly yet again and his features hardened in anger. Her control slipping, Allie fired her own wrath to light, tearing into him unmindful of betraying her jealousy. 'I don't want to hear it. So you were married to a paragon of womanly talent and now you've found another one in Elaine! Well, bully for you!'

'Is that why you think I told you about Natalie? Because I want another wife like her and I want that wife to be *Elaine*?' His anger vanished, replaced by astonishment. 'Listen to me, Allie,' he demanded, coming over to catch her by the shoulders. She tried to twist free but he held her firm. At his touch, the dam that was holding back her tears burst and they flowed down her cheeks. 'I am not marrying Elaine. I don't want to and I have never wanted to marry Elaine.'

In her distress, Allie wasn't immediately cognisant of what he had said. He pulled her against his hard chest, cradling her head firmly against his shoulder. 'I am *not* marrying Elaine, you silly girl,' he reassured her. His hand ran over the smooth satin of her hair, imparting comfort. 'I don't know where you get your crazy ideas, but that one is way off-base. I've known Elaine for a long time, but I honestly have never even thought of her that way. I've taken her around a bit, because she doesn't make friends easily and doesn't have much of a social life, but that's all that has ever been between us.'

There was no denying the sincerity in his voice, and it soothed away her fears. Quiet against his chest now, Allie felt weak-kneed with relief. She'd been so sure that was what he had come to tell her. The temptation to linger in his arms was overpowering, but after a moment he eased her away from him and peered down into her tear-washed eyes. 'Now that that is straightened out, will you let me finish telling you what I have to say?'

Allie looked up at him, her grey eyes wide and vulnerable. She wanted only to go back into his embrace, to be held against him without explanations. A cold trickle of apprehension slid down her spine. She didn't *want* to hear any explanations. He'd told her when he first came in that he had sent her away because he didn't think that it could ever work between them. Nothing had really changed.

She stepped back from him and he let his arms fall to his side. 'I'm not like your first wife, Linc. I don't think that I could ever be like her. I'm just not cut out to be the *hausfrau*.'

'I don't want you to be,' Linc said with emphasis. 'You didn't let me finish talking the first time. I loved Natalie when we first got married, but by the time she died . . . I was upset, of course, but in a way it got me out of a marriage that I wasn't happy in. We never argued, but we had absolutely nothing in common in the end, except Jason. I wanted more from a marriage partner than just good food, a clean house, and a warm bed. To put it bluntly, Natalie bored me.'

He moved over to Allie, not taking her in his arms, but gently laying his hands on her shoulders. 'I drove you away because even though I knew I was in love with you, I was afraid that if we continued in our relationship it would go the way things did in my first marriage. I'm still a little afraid of that.'

'I don't understand,' Allie admitted, shaking her head. 'What are you afraid of? That you'll tire of me? I just told you I'm not like your late wife, I'm not domesticated. I . . .'

Before she could continue, there was a discreet knock at the door. They both glanced towards it, then Linc released her, saying, 'I suppose you had better see who it is.'

Allie nodded, going quickly to answer the summons. Whoever was calling had picked an inauspicious moment to do so, and they'd get little welcome from her.

It was only a bellboy, however. 'Dr Smith?' he asked, and she nodded. 'This message was left for you at the desk.' He handed over the white envelope and she accepted it.

'Just a moment.' Retrieving her bag, she found the boy a tip, then sent him on his way. The door closed, she leaned against it and glanced down at the unopened envelope. The prosaic interruption had recalled her to the details of ordinary life. She glanced at her watch. 'Damn, my meeting was supposed to have started ten minutes ago,' she said distractedly, not looking up at Linc as she tore the envelope open.

'Oh, good . . . it's been post . . . poned.' The last word was drawn out as she read the signature on the message. For the first time since opening the door, she looked at Linc, her eyes startled. '*You're* Aragon Software?'

'And you are Dr A. Jennings Smith,' Linc stated grimly, his voice a blend of astonishment and anger.

His tone jolted her, and she eyed him warily. She hadn't even thought about Linc's still regarding her as the air-headed dimwit she'd pretended to be last summer. Carelessly, she had given herself away now without preparing him—and obviously he wasn't too pleased with her. Little drifts of crimson rage were creeping up his cheeks, and his eyes couldn't have been harder if they'd been made of stone.

Striving to pass it over, Allie answered lightly, 'Well, of course I am.' He didn't reply. 'Surely you knew that?' She laughed softly, but to no avail. No answering smile touched his mouth. Cornered, Allie went on the offensive. 'I told you I had an appointment. Why didn't *you* let me know it was with you so I wouldn't have been worrying about missing it?'

'*My* appointment, which I put off, was with A. Jennings Smith, B.Sc., M.Sc., Ph.D. We were going to discuss the new software package he, or rather *she*, had developed for the fish-farming industry.' His gaze slid down her figure with insulting intent. 'I certainly never imagined that *Dr* Smith was the dumb blonde I'd met last summer.'

'You mean, Clare didn't tell you?' Allie attempted, quailing slightly under his towering rage.

'No, Clare didn't tell me!' he mimicked snidely. 'You two really must have laughed yourself silly at the fool you made out of me.' He pushed past her, heading for the door.

'Yes, just get the hell out of here!' Allie shouted at him. 'You're just like every other man I ever met. You can't stand the idea that I might be smarter than you are!'

'There you've got it wrong, lady,' he shot back, swinging back around to confront her. 'With all your vast IQ, can't you figure out why I dumped you last summer? I cut you out of my life because I thought you were so dumb you'd bore me silly if we ever got married! That's where your stupid little game got us!'

They glared at one another, two antagonists facing one another in mortal combat. Suddenly, though, the bubble of Allie's anger burst, shattering her. 'You thought I was too dumb to be your wife?' she asked in a whisper.

'That's right, too dumb,' he confirmed, his voice subsiding to a normal level as his fury subsided. They stared at one another for a full minute, then one corner of Linc's mouth suddenly twitched upwards. Allie saw the movement, and a giggle rose in her throat.

'You thought I was too dumb,' she repeated, her laughter breaking free to be joined by his.

'Yes, *Dr* Smith, I guess I'm a hard man to please,' he advised her through his mirth. When eventually they gained control of their hilarity, Linc sobered. 'I was afraid of making the same mistake I did in my first marriage. Natalie . . . I couldn't talk to her. She couldn't understand half of what I tried to explain to her, so I finally gave up. We just sort of drifted along after that, going our separate ways.'

'I . . . I . . .' She shook her head. 'I thought you wouldn't want anything to do with me if you knew I was . . .'

'A brain?' he supplied. He smiled, and it was as if the sun had come out after a thunderstorm. 'It was just the opposite. I tried to get you interested in my work, but you didn't seem to understand any of it.'

Allie nibbled her lower lip, then confessed, 'Actually, I was very interested. In fact, that night you were telling me about the program you were developing—later, I looked up the company that was producing that new echo-sounder you told me about. I used data from it to develop my fish-count program.'

'You did?' he asked, considering for a moment. 'So that's how you've managed to get such accuracy.' He gave her a long look, his features demanding, but there was a gentle light in his eyes. 'And what about chess? Do you really not know how to play?'

'I know how,' she admitted sheepishly, flushing pink. 'I've collected a few master points, in fact.'

His eyebrows rose. 'I really ought to beat you for deceiving me like you did,' he said sternly. Despite his tone, when he walked over to her, his arms were gentle as they encircled her willing form. His lips took hers in a warm, tender kiss. When he lifted his head, he murmured, 'What were we arguing about?' Unable to get enough of the taste of her, his lips lingered over her cheek, her temple.

'I don't remember,' Allie breathed, tightening her arms about his waist to pull him closer. She moved against him provocatively, her mouth parted in invitation.

He denied her, however. Although his arms

remained around her, he put a space between them so that he could look down into her eyes. 'Did you really think I wouldn't love you if I thought you were too intelligent.'

Avoiding his gaze, Allie nodded slightly and felt him tense.

'Can't say I care much for your assessment of my character,' he admitted sardonically.

'You have to understand,' Allie explained, smoothing down his ruffled feathers. 'That's been men's usual reaction to me in the past . . . all except for one.'

'The man you were involved with before coming out to Vancouver Island? Tell me about him. Did you love him?'

There was a faint note of jealousy in his voice that thrilled her, but she wanted to allay it none the less. 'Not really.' She went on to tell him all that had happened with Kevin.

'He sounds like a jerk,' Linc pronounced dismissively at the end, but she heard relief in his voice. They kissed again, then Linc pulled away. 'I hope you're not going to think that the only reason *I* am marrying you is to get hold of your fish-count program. I will admit that I'd be pretty upset if you sold it to anyone else.'

Allie's eyes were misted with happiness as she looked up at him. 'Are we getting married?'

'Of course we are. The minute I saw you again in that elevator, I knew I had to stop kidding myself. Dumb blonde or not, I knew I couldn't let you slip away from me again.'

'How would you like a program for counting fish as a wedding present?'

He gave her a glance of wry charm. 'That doesn't sound very romantic. Besides, I won't let you. You may be a whiz at maths and science, but you don't appear to

know much about business. That program could make
you a fortune.'

'Really?' Allie exclaimed, drawing back to peer into
his face. He nodded. 'I thought I'd only get a few
thousand dollars for it.'

'If it does what you claim it does, you'd better be
adding some zeros on that estimate, my dear.'

'Oh.' She gave him a disconcerted look. 'I don't know
much about the marketing end of things. This was the
first time I've tried to sell a freelance project. In fact, I
was scared about having to meet with . . . I guess it was
you,' she laughed softly.

'Well, you're just lucky it *was* me. Someone else might
have been tempted to take you to the cleaners, but I
pride myself on Aragon Software's making a profit
without having to take advantage of people.'

Her grin was pert. 'I won't worry about that. I think
I'll let my husband deal with all my business in the
future.'

'I guess that would be a solution,' he laughed.
Bending his head to claim her mouth again, they were
interrupted by the jangling of the telephone. 'Damn,' he
said, releasing her.

'We could let it ring,' Allie suggested, but glanced
over to the offending instrument. Her gaze caught on
the bedside clock: five past eight. 'Oh, no!' she
exclaimed. 'I'm supposed to give a talk tonight at eight
o'clock. I haven't even changed!' She gave Linc a look of
helpless distress.

'Calm down,' Linc advised, striding over to the phone
and lifting the receiver. 'Yes, Dr Smith is here
. . . yes, yes. Well there's been a delay, but she'll be
along in a few minutes.' He replaced the receiver and
turned back to where Allie was standing passively in the
centre of the room. 'That was the conference organisers.

They're wondering what's happened to you.'

'Oh, hell! This is always happening to me!' Allie swore, feeling dreadful and ashamed at having let the conference organisers down. 'I don't suppose they'll ever ask me back.'

'They will. After all, you have a good excuse for being late . . . unless you get engaged every day?'

She grinned at him suddenly. 'I don't.' Like a homing pigeon, she headed for his arms again, but he stopped her.

'None of that,' he chided. 'I promised them I'd have you there in a few minutes. Now, have you got your notes for your talk prepared?'

'They're in my briefcase,' she admitted, reluctantly going to fetch it. Her nerves were rock-steady now—she just didn't want to leave Linc to give her talk. She'd rather stay here and have him make love to her.

'Stop dallying,' Linc disciplined her, taking the briefcase from her. 'I'll dig out your notes while you go do whatever you have to with your hair and make-up.'

'But my dress! It's too casual,' Allie protested. 'I haven't time to change it. Couldn't we just call them and tell them I've died!'

He chuckled at her suggestion, but none the less started rummaging through the papers in her case, looking for the appropriate pages. 'You don't want to cheat me out of my moment of glory, do you?'

'What do you mean?'

Finding the notes at last, he walked over to her, planting a firm kiss on her mouth. 'I mean that every man there is going to be envying the fellow who's captured the most beautiful, brilliant woman in the world. And I'm that fellow!' Turning her towards the bathroom, he gave her a little shove. 'Now, go gild the lily a little bit and we'll be on our way.'

*   *   *

The delegates to the annual convention of the National Association of Computer Programmers and Analysts stirred restlessly in their seats as they waited for the main speaker of the evening session to arrive. At last there was a flurry of movement at the stage door, and a young girl with flyaway blonde hair and sparkling grey eyes emerged on to the stage. There was a general sigh of disgruntlement. She was probably the eminent Dr Smith's secretary, here to tell them that the delay would be prolonged.

However, the master of ceremonies for the evening greeted the girl with relief—his small store of anecdotes to keep the crowd amused having been depleted—and turned to face the audience.

'Distinguished colleagues, I give you our speaker for the evening, Dr A. Jennings Smith.'

Allie stepped up to the podium and waited for the man who had just entered the auditorium to take his seat in the front row. The shy smile that flitted across her lips was solely for his benefit. He returned it with one of his own, a smile of pride and encouragement. Linc raised his thumb in a thumbs-up signal and, leaning back in his seat, crossed his arms in front of him, relishing the coming moments. Before launching into her opening remarks, Allie saw him turn his head to say a word to the man seated next to him. The distinguished gentleman looked hard at Linc, then up at her. Hiding a grin, Allie looked down at her notes. She guessed the man *had* looked faintly envious after hearing what Linc had told him. Lifting her head with an upsurge of self-confidence, Allie began to speak.

HARLEQUIN
Romance®

Coming Next Month

Available in February wherever paperback books are sold, or through
Harlequin Reader Service:

In the U.S.
901 Fuhrmann Blvd.
P.O. Box 1397
Buffalo, N.Y. 14240-1397

In Canada
P.O. Box 603
Fort Erie, Ontario
L2A 5X3

A compelling novel of deadly revenge and passion
from Harlequin's bestselling international
romance author Penny Jordan

POWER PLAY

Eleven years had passed but the
terror of that night was something
Pepper Minesse would never
forget. Fueled by revenge against
the four men who had brutally
shattered her past, she set in
motion a deadly plan to destroy
their futures.

Available in February!

 Harlequin Books®

HPP-1A

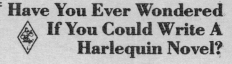

Have You Ever Wondered If You Could Write A Harlequin Novel?

Here's great news—Harlequin is offering a series of cassette tapes to help you do just that. Written by Harlequin editors, these tapes give practical advice on how to make your characters—and your story—come alive. There's a tape for each contemporary romance series Harlequin publishes.

Mail order only

All sales final

TO: **Harlequin Reader Service**
Audiocassette Tape Offer
P.O. Box 1396
Buffalo, NY 14269-1396

I enclose a check/money order payable to HARLEQUIN READER SERVICE® for $9.70 ($8.95 plus 75¢ postage and handling) for EACH tape ordered for the total sum of $_____ *
Please send:

☐ Romance and Presents   ☐ Intrigue
☐ American Romance   ☐ Temptation
☐ Superromance   ☐ All five tapes ($38.80 total)

Signature_____
                                    (please print clearly)
Name:_____
Address:_____
State:_____ Zip:_____

*Iowa and New York residents add appropriate sales tax.

                                                AUDIO-H

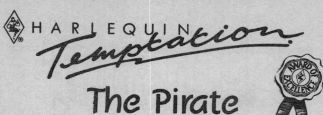

The Pirate
JAYNE ANN KRENTZ

At the heart of every powerful romance story lies a legend. There are many romantic legends and countless modern variations on them, but they all have one thing in common: They are tales of brave, resourceful women who must gentle and tame the powerful, passionate men who are their true mates.

The enormous appeal of Jayne Ann Krentz lies in her ability to create modern-day versions of these classic romantic myths, and her LADIES AND LEGENDS trilogy showcases this talent. Believing that a storyteller who can bring legends to life deserves special attention, Harlequin has chosen the first book of the trilogy—THE PIRATE—to receive our Award of Excellence. Look for it in February.

AE-PIR-1

Step into a world of pulsing adventure, gripping emotion and lush sensuality with these evocative love stories penned by today's bestselling authors in the highest romantic tradition. Pursuing their passionate dreams against a backdrop of the past's most colorful and dramatic moments, our vibrant heroines and dashing heroes will make history come alive for you.

Watch for new Harlequin Historicals each month, available wherever Harlequin Books are sold.

History has never been so romantic!

GHIST-1R